IT WAS LIKE THIS

Also by Anne Goodwin Winslow
The Dwelling Place
A Winter in Green
Cloudy Trophies
A Quiet Neighborhood
The Springs

IT WAS LIKE THIS

ANNE GOODWIN WINSLOW

CUTTING EDGE

ISBN-13: 978-1-957868-70-7

Published by
Cutting Edge Books
PO Box 8212
Calabasas, CA 91372
www.cuttingedgebooks.com

PART ONE

NUTWOOD

CHAPTER ONE

WHEN THE MARTINS built their house in a pecan grove and named it quite frankly Nutwood, it was without any direct intention of selling nuts. They had naturally expected to have more of them than they could use themselves or even give to the neighbors, who probably had trees of their own, in which case the only reasonable thing to do would be to sell them—in southern Mississippi after the close of the Civil War it was reasonable to sell almost anything—but pecans as a source of income had not occurred to them. It came as a surprise that anything could be so bountiful and so marketable at the same time—those two qualities having as a rule a nullifying effect on each other. It almost seemed as if there might be a tide in nuts which taken at the flood might lead the Martins on—not to fortune exactly, but nearer to it than either beans or strawberries promised to do.

In the twenty-odd years that had passed since they made this discovery the big gray trees on the lawn had grown bigger and shaggier but not less prodigal of their fruit, and now on the other side of the lane that ran by the house and led off into the fields a plantation of new trees was bearing. They stood in long rows, silvery and slender; there was something virginal about their aspect, especially without their leaves. They seemed to spend more time without their leaves than trees were supposed to do in that gentle latitude; they always stripped first and shivered longest.

Hugh Martin, who was walking in the lane and making these reflections not for the first time, regarded this callow forest without admiration. He could remember when it was planted; he must have been about seven; and even then he had not liked the idea of trees in rows; especially naked trees. It was now only the beginning of November, and there they stood without a stitch already.

Hugh had arrived the evening before and was himself noticeably well-dressed; well-dressed for the country; he had always hated to see city clothes where they did not belong, even in the days when he had not had any and only saw them on other people. He did not bring the ones he had now, when he came home. He was a young man rather below than above the middle height and not too slender, but almost too graceful in his movements to suggest a physical superiority that he had none the less made a point of cultivating and had at present little opportunity to enjoy—but which he did bring when he came back to the country. He was walking at present with a direct stride in which there was an indication of a slight limp, never noticeable in his ordinary step and so little a part of the careless ease of everything else about him that hardly anyone ever remembered it. "Have you hurt yourself?" he was sometimes asked perfunctorily, and the answer, or no answer, was as likely as not unheeded.

It was not yet seven in the morning and as usual at that hour a light mist hung over the landscape, softening without embellishment the outlines of everything. It was not, Hugh thought, a prospect that needed softening; it had no salient features. The house, maybe, with all those excrescences—he had turned and was walking back toward the house—but the morning dimness did not help that either. He pulled out his watch. He hated to be up early for no other reason than not being able to sleep late. The country always kept him awake until he got used to it. He turned from the lane into the yard, closing the gate—a small one made of green palings like the fence—noiselessly behind him. There were three people presumably asleep in the house: his mother, his brother, and his brother's wife. His brother had been married for nearly three years now, but he knew if the latch clicked and she came to the window—Would he never get used to the idea of Anna being there in Lawrence's room? Standing, his hand on the gate, he looked up at the window, wide open to the misty air. Its white curtains hung motionless; they framed no face.

There were many windows. The house though not beautiful was spacious; built of native pine, once painted green to match the fence and no doubt with the idea of matching the trees as well. The fence had renewed its color more than once since then, as had the trees, but the house, although still spoken of as green, had weathered to a blend of woodland tints that could hardly have been given a name though it might have been thought charming.

It had been built in one of the bad periods of domestic architecture, but with many comfortable features that a lack of money had been instrumental in preserving through subsequent improvements in taste. The Martins' taste, however, had not improved any to speak of—except in the case of Hugh, who had been away from home a great deal more than the rest of them. Hugh had presumably learned about such matters enough to appreciate them; too much, the others sometimes thought, to appreciate their relative unimportance. It was staying in the country year in and year out, and especially making your living out of it, that taught you that; it taught you a different set of values—or rather to keep the ones you had. Hugh had discovered new ones.

"What in the world makes you get up like this?" his mother asked him when he came into the dining-room, where breakfast was ready at last. "I sent Eva in more than an hour ago to fix you a fire, and you were already up and out." Mrs. Martin was seated at the head of the table, a fire of pitch pine blazing beautifully in the chimney behind her; facing her were two long windows opening on the east, but she was lighted principally by Hugh, coming in at the side.

"And what in the world makes you think I want a fire, Mamma? Don't start making company of me when you know you can't keep it up." He took the place at her right—the company place. "And don't you fix me any more fires to dress by, Eva; not unless it snows." This pleasantry he exchanged for the hot biscuit Eva was handing him. "Lordy, it's nice to be here!" he said, looking around contentedly. "But I thought farmers had to get up." He glanced at the two empty places.

"You ought to have been here a couple of weeks ago," his mother said. "This is just an interval."

Hugh looked through the open door into the hall. "I know about those intervals," he said. There were footsteps coming down the stairs.

"What in the world makes you get up like this?" It was Lawrence's turn to ask the question. He pushed Anna's chair in for her and pulled out his own. "We thought one of the dogs had got left in the house; Anna wanted me to get up and let you out."

"But then I remembered.—Thank you, Eva," Anna said, taking her cup.

"Remembered that I had come?"

"That you couldn't sleep when you first came. I believe it's going to be a pretty day." She looked out dispassionately on the day, and Hugh looked dispassionately at her. Not white and gold as he persistently remembered her; she had not been that since she was little and was made to wear her hat; having spent the intervening years mostly without it, she was now beautifully weathered, like the house. Her hair, about the color that her hat used to be, was combed back from a brow no longer pale and gathered into a low knot on a neck that had ceased to resemble that of a snow maiden. Her eyes, which had been blue, light blue, were darker now and only blue when she had on a blue dress. She was lovely. She would always be lovely. "Just leave me one little bone, if I can't have anything else." He had said that to her once. What a fool.

"Has Hugh noticed your cap?" Anna said as Mrs. Martin rose from the table.

"I don't know. Have you, Hugh?" His mother faced him.

"Of course," he said. "But I didn't know why you were wearing it. You aren't old or anything, are you?"

"I don't know whether I am or not. You are supposed to wear the things if you live to be fifty. I've held out longer than that."

Anna got up and went around the table to adjust the cap, taking a small hairpin from her own head to tuck back a lock that had strayed from under the edge of black lace. "But you do think it's becoming to her, don't you, Hugh?" she asked him.

"Hurry up and say so, Hugh, so she can take it off," Lawrence said. "It cripples you terribly, don't it, Mamma?"

"In the garden it does; it gets caught on things," Mrs. Martin said. "Yesterday I went back to look for it and found it hung up in the crab-apple tree—like Absalom."

Lawrence laughed. Standing by his mother, a rather long, rather loose young man in outdoor clothes, his resemblance to her, always striking, was not lessened even by the cap; it had held its own through worse disguises. It was the sort of likeness that is apt to be openly commented on—a convenient vestibule to conversation, and one that led most people to the inference that the other son, since he looked like neither one of them, must "take after the other side." But this, it seemed, was a mistake. There were two or three small photographs of Mr. Martin in the family album—a young man with a pleated shirt-front and a loose black cravat—a still younger man wearing a belt and sword: presentments of a type rather than an individual, and looking so little like anybody in particular that they could hardly be expected to look like Hugh. His mother did not expect it; she had known from his babyhood that it was her father, not his own, that Hugh had chosen to resemble, and had approved the choice. She had loved her husband and gone with him unfalteringly into the shadows that had engulfed their world, but her father's star had set in different skies and she saw it rise again in Hugh.

"Is anybody going to the post office?" Anna asked, looking out again on the clearing sky. "I'll finish my letter."

"I'm going," Hugh said.

"Want your horse? Andy will catch him for you." Lawrence started toward the kitchen.

"That's right; tell Andy to catch the company's horse," Hugh said. "Is it two days or only one that he does that? Anyhow he needn't count today. I'm walking; I'll get the boat."

It was nearly two miles by the road to Pass Christian, where the post office was, but less than half that distance to the beach where the boat was kept. One could see the long pale ribbon of the Sound over the treetops from the upstairs windows, and almost see the boat, tied to the little rickety dock or pulled up on the sand. *Anita* was the name painted on it, but that was no longer visible except at very close range. Nobody used the boat these days but John Coujac, who owned the dock; he was supposed to look after the *Anita* and to go fishing in her when he felt like it: presumably when he was hungry.

"If he has been out this morning you might bring some mullet for lunch," Mrs. Martin suggested. "I know you never get any really fresh fish in Richmond."

A stale place Richmond; his family continually reminded him of all he lost by living in an inland city. His sea-breathing family—Hugh wondered as he walked through the wood to the beach how long it had been since any one of them, even Lawrence, had taken this path. They never even went where they could see the water, or had any connection with it closer than eating fish. That was the biggest difference between him and Lawrence—their feeling about the Sound. They got started wrong; Lawrence probably got discouraged when he was little, trying to keep up with a brother three years older; not only about swimming but a lot of things. Three years made a big difference when they were almost all the years you had. Not in the way they felt about each other, but the way they felt about practically everything else—everything they wanted to do. Those were the lines of cleavage between children growing up; especially boys—the things they couldn't do together, either because they didn't both like them, or maybe once in a while because they both did; that last was the worst of course. He and Lawrence had both wanted to marry Anna—that was inevitable; that was, so to speak, written, from the day their mother brought her to live with them—but even so there was as big a difference in the way they used to feel about Anna as there was in anything.

A turn in the road brought an end to the wooded part of it. It suddenly became nothing but a rather unkempt strip of shore with here and there a small unsheltered house stranded on it like a shell. The dock and the *Anita* were in the immediate foreground. The *Anita* had been pulled up on the sand and a little farther along John Coujac's two-room house might be said also to have been pulled up; far enough presumably to be out of the reach of storms, or at least the general run of them. His family, which had at one time something more than filled it, being now all gone, he had this habitation to himself, and in the patch of shade that slanted off from it was at the moment cleaning fish in an expert and inattentive manner that left his eyes, and no doubt his thoughts too, free to wander. They lighted on Hugh with no indication of surprise; his comings and goings, though sometimes months apart, had acquired an accepted place in the general shiftiness of John Coujac's outlook—his wavering skyline and his elusive fish, to say nothing of his family. In appearance he was as usual sad and slack, but Hugh did not believe he was thinking of his family.

"I'm rowing over to the Pass," he called to him as he turned down toward the boat. "Save me some of those, will you? My mother wants them for lunch."

"A'right," John Coujac answered, following him with his eyes across the pale field of vision made by sand and sea, then reverting to his fish.

"He's never given a damn about anything since he was born," Hugh reflected, pushing the *Anita* off. "And he looks exactly the way he did when I first remember him. The fountain of Juventus—that's the secret of it: letting things go—go where they can't hurt him, instead of holding on to them, even the broken ones; cutting himself on spilled milk, as Jackson would say." Jackson wrote editorials for the *Richmond Democrat,* but observed no other verbal allegiance. It was that paper, duly forwarded—milk spilled day before yesterday—that Hugh was on his way to the post office to get.

The morning had not yet altogether emerged from its misty beginning. November was like that down here; a reticent clarity that didn't promise anything special, nor claim any particular attention; rather restful after the Virginia autumn. The Sound between the mainland and the long flat edge of the islands lying farther out was not much broader than a river and every bit as still. He kept the boat in close to the shore where John Coujac's house and the one or two others like it had now given place to the live-oaks and the wide white road that made the charming waterfront of the little town. Everybody's front gate opened on the shell road; everybody's house was set back from it at varying distances, variously adorned with shrubs and flowers. Here was color of the kind that did claim attention; beds of roses still in bloom, and the scarlet hibiscus on Mrs. Middleton's lawn blooming already. Many of the houses were built in the New Orleans fashion, with open arches underneath and wrought-iron balustrades. They had a graceful foreign air at variance with the foursquare aspect of the typical Southern colonial; yet they represented something solid too, in the sense that it had altered little through the years. Hugh remembered two or three places where he ought to stop before he went home—after he got his mail. His mother's old friends always liked to inaugurate his return. He would leave Mrs. Middleton for the last.

A fire burned softly at one end of the long room in which Mrs. Middleton sat, but she was sitting at the other end, by the window, where she could see her red hibiscus on the lawn; where she had no doubt seen Hugh, tying his boat at the steps of the pier, like Venice, and coming through the gate. That was nearly an hour ago; she knew it was time for him to be reversing the process now, or he would be late for lunch. He had declined her invitation to stay to lunch with her, but he had taken the last little cake from the coffee table between them and was eating it slowly.

She looked over at the chair where he had put his hat with the newspapers under it. "What's in your old *Democrat*?" she asked him. "What are you giving those people up there to think about these days—besides politics?"

"What is there besides politics?"

"Well, there are always the politicians—who haven't any; those commanders of the faithful without any faith. Not that they are worth writing about either. Unless you have to, of course. Poor Hugh! How much longer is it going to be journalism? Your ideas are too good for that sort of desultory writing. Why don't you do something more sustained—more imaginative—say a novel?"

"Why should I, if my ideas are so good? In that case they ought to be able to stand up and fight in their own skins, and not have to be dressed up like men and women, wouldn't you think so?"

"All the same, I was talking to Noel about it when he was here for Thanksgiving—"

"What did he say?"

"Oh, he was listening; he doesn't answer back the way you do; I raised him better. But go ahead and read me what you have been saying."

He knew as well as she did that he ought to be going, instead of sitting down again and starting in on newspapers. But who else was there around here who cared anything about his work—even the little that Mrs. Middleton cared—even enough to tell him that she didn't care for it at all? He unfolded day before yesterday's *Democrat* and located his own column. Whether she liked what he wrote or not, she always saw the point, if there was one.

Mrs. Middleton had never been considered pretty, even in her youth; Hugh had often heard his mother comment on the fact that she didn't have the looks she was entitled to—that went in her family, and had gone to some extent into the portraits of her family with which it was customary to compare her. One of them hung behind her chair, where Hugh might have compared her now; only he never could; he couldn't see her out of that plum-colored dress she wore in the morning, except to see her in the black silk one she wore in the evening; he couldn't see her holding flowers, or a fan. The lady behind her had both; she was young, of course, but Mrs. Middleton didn't even have her knitting. He didn't believe she owned any knitting; there was nothing to punctuate her.

"—So you see," he said when he had finished, "what the brilliant journalist needs is not ideas but references. 'As the dean of St. Patrick's observed—' and from there on I just hand the story over to Jonathan Swift and let him tell it in his own words; I don't even have to bother to write like him. Nothing delights a reader as much as to recognize a reference; it doesn't have to be literary. It can be geographical, military, Masonic—any old friend of his youth."

Mrs. Middleton laughed. "And I suppose you always have an appropriate old friend on hand?"

"They are all appropriate sooner or later. A reference naturally refers to something, and there isn't anything that doesn't happen over again. Everything keeps coming back, if you look on long enough."

She shook her head. "Not for me it doesn't. People say that, but I've been looking on a mighty long time. I'm a monument, Hugh, with the procession passing—"

"And not repeating itself?"

"No: always being different. That's the discouraging thing about the human spectacle; it hasn't any pattern—any meaning; there are not enough people who are like each other, or who even stay like themselves."

Hugh laughed. "You are like Trinity College: you have seen 'Wordsworth drunk and Porson sober,' haven't you? But a monument does have a meaning; drunk or sober we all look up to you."

"That's nice, Hugh," she said. "I wonder sometimes if Richmond appreciates you." She looked at him thoughtfully.

"I saw Anna the other day," she said after a while. "She gets prettier all the time. Noel was here; he said if she keeps on, in another ten years she will be the most beautiful woman in the world."

"Out of it, he means. How much of the world does he think Anna's beauty will permeate, even in ten years? There aren't any topless towers around here for her to set fire to."

"No, I suppose not," Mrs. Middleton said and was again silent, while Hugh folded Wednesday's paper up again and opened Tuesday's, giving it the dark-browed attention he habitually bestowed on anything that interested him. As if it had bad news in it, she thought, instead of something he had written himself. He had been like that when he was little—if you gave him anything to play with, or to eat, he would glower at it first and smile up at you afterwards. It was a sign of feeling, no doubt, but an unfortunate one. He had probably glowered at Anna a good deal, first and last. It was a queer thing, Mrs. Middleton reflected, that she had known those children of Louisa Martin's all their lives—all the part of it they could remember, at any rate—and yet she knew almost as little about what had gone on between them as a stranger would have known. And nobody had been secretive either, or even shy. Just good manners all round—or what went for good manners in their part of the world. Ask me no questions and I'll tell you no lies, as the darkies said. All the same, there were a few things she would like to know. Certainly there was one while, and not a short while either—there had been several years there when everything pointed to Hugh as the one who was going to marry Anna. Louisa Martin had pointed to him herself—without knowing she was doing it. It was because things had changed between Hugh and Anna—and without either questions or lies Mrs. Middleton did know something about what had changed them—that Hugh had gone to Richmond and started writing on the paper—

"Just listen to this," he said. "Old Jackson can be good sometimes." His smile, which was—or was by contrast—so much more than a smile that it always surprised her, surprised her now; old Jackson's coruscations were lost in its peculiar radiance. She remembered telling his mother once that what went on in Hugh's face, to say nothing of his voice, was an emotional experience for the bystander, whatever it might be to him. It was heredity, Louisa had explained simply. "My father could sway thousands of people from tears to laughter without seeming to know he was doing it." So Mrs. Middleton sat now under the spell of heredity and listened to the *Democrat;* part of her mind on what Hugh was reading, but most of it on him.

She had always been sure he was Louisa's favorite of the two boys—whether Louisa knew that or not. No mother ever admitted having a favorite child, but they all did—provided they had as many as two. The most brilliant one, if one of them happened to be brilliant, or maybe just the worst one, if he was bad in an interesting way. There was always a dramatic element to be considered in that mother-love business; and in Louisa's case there was her own father-love mixed in with it—all that heredity idea. She seemed to think Hugh was going to take up right where his grandfather left off, with no allowance made for anything that had happened in the meanwhile. What was it somebody said about the velvet and bright iron of the past?—It was a pity there couldn't be a little money along with the rest of the heredity. But even there—Louisa never seemed to grasp the difference between being sent to an English university, the way her father was, and poor Hugh scrambling for an education down in New Orleans, working all day and studying all night. Just so he got the education, Louisa thought. She had a great regard for the classics; her father had swayed them too. And all the while Lawrence was there at home running the place and being taken for granted. He was only supposed to look like his mother, as he did of course; but his mind was every bit as good as Hugh's—in its own way. Lawrence was delightful; there was a great harmony there, a great charm. Anna had probably felt it more than they realized; it was a steady influence in her life, going on all that time Hugh was being so tempestuous about her; she may have been drawn into it as the thing she needed most. Peace—it was hard to imagine a girl choosing peace instead of love—with her eyes open. But had Anna's eyes ever been open to love?

The lunch bell was ringing as Hugh came across the lawn with his string of fish. His mother and Anna were coming out of the garden, where they had evidently been gathering things. Mrs. Martin's gray locks, now capless, were straying in the wind; she was flushed and happy.

"Am I late?" Hugh looked down apologetically at the mullet.

"Yes, but don't bother; they will do for supper. I hope you told John Coujac we would be wanting them often while you are here. Oysters too."

"Oh, I'll be going out with him. The old boy looked sort of lonesome. I always forget about there being nobody there any more. Mrs. Middleton sent you both her love," he went on, looking at Anna, who was walking ahead.

The wind had not ruffled Anna's hair; it was as smoothly shining as a petal or a leaf. Her dress, of some unbleached material, brushed the grass, and being herself unbleached, even a little burnished, she gave the effect of having been cut all out of one piece, like a statue. To Hugh the impression was not a new one; he had labored under it—he had wallowed in it—considerably in the past; it was one of her mythological aspects. He recalled a poem he had written to it—recalled the whole thing with no effort at all: "Diana of the Ephesians." Demetrius the silversmith was speaking—

> *That her temple should not be despised*
> *And her magnificence destroyed,*
> *Whom all Asia worshippeth—*

What a fool.

"I am glad you went to see Mrs. Middleton, Hugh," his mother said at the lunch table. "I hoped you would. Did she tell you any news?"

"All there was. She thinks Noel is in love—if you call that news. He didn't happen to mention it to you, did he, Anna?"

"As a matter of fact, he did," Anna said; "though of course it may not be the same girl his mother was thinking of. He liked something of yours he had been reading, Hugh—something about Macaulay. He says you are 'arriving.'"

"Coming in on Macaulay's shoulders," Hugh said.

"We haven't told him about us yet, have we?" Anna looked across at Lawrence. "We are arriving too."

"What are they talking about?" Hugh asked his mother.

"I thought they wanted to show it to you first," Mrs. Martin said. "Go on and tell him, Lawrence."

"I was going to take him out there this afternoon," Lawrence said.

"Out where?"

"To the Duncan place. Anna and I have bought the Duncan place," Lawrence told him.

"What for?" Hugh looked from one of them to the other.

"We want to get rich," Anna said. "Lawrence has the most wonderful project. You remember the big spring out there? It is right at the head of a hollow where we can build a dam with hardly any trouble at all, Lawrence thinks, and have a lake—or a pond, Lawrence calls it."

"What for?" Hugh said again.

"So we can irrigate—so we won't have to be always at the mercy of the weather," Anna explained. "Lawrence thinks we can irrigate any number of acres of anything we decide to plant, but the main thing we are thinking about right now is tomatoes. Have you ever heard of the Rubiglobe tomato, Hugh? We want to try all the new varieties. We are coming in on Burpee's shoulders."

Hugh looked at her. All this volubility—all this animation— it took something like a tomato every time to quicken Anna's latent fires. Then she could sing. Few but roses.

"I hope they are not making a mistake," Mrs. Martin said. "As far as the land is concerned, I hardly see how it could fail to be a good investment; but all this hydraulic business sounds terribly expensive. And it's Anna's money—"

"Yes, and who has been saving it for her all these years," Anna broke in—"and never let her spend a cent of it on anybody but herself? And now we are going to enjoy it! Don't listen to her, Hugh. Just watch her when we get out the catalogues and start making our lists. You'll see!"

"I'm not going to listen to any of you very much until I know a little better what you are talking about," Hugh said. "Eva certainly hasn't forgotten her apple pie, has she?" He smiled and shook his head at the "one more slice" his mother was balancing on the pie-knife. "Whistle when you are ready, Lawrence; I'll be writing a few letters."

It was a short afternoon—now in November—but when Lawrence, leaning down from his saddle, closed the gate of the Duncan place behind them, Hugh felt that he had been taken farther back into the past, than he had counted on going. Not that they had mentioned it particularly; they had talked principally about the Duncan place, which he hardly remembered in the past and was now being asked to consider in the future—Lawrence's future; not his; the thing he and Lawrence had together was their past, and when they got off alone this way, which had not happened much of late, that was where they went.

"And I know one thing—" Lawrence had fastened the gate now and caught up with him—"if we hadn't done this we would have done something else just like it. Anna simply won't hear to an investment that she can't see—is the way she puts it. There is nothing intrinsic about 'shares,' she says. And of course Mamma agrees with her. It's a funny thing for a girl whose family, as far as she knows anything about them, have never lived in the country, to feel about it the way she does; not just æsthetically, but right down to the roots. I don't see where she gets it."

"Still, you can't imagine her in a city very much," Hugh said. "I can't." They were on their way home now; Anna was rising between them.

"And yet—" Lawrence began.

"And yet what will she—what will you both do with the money after you have made it? More tomatoes? Even a tomato stops being intrinsic when you start multiplying it by a thousand bushels, it seems to me."

"That's just it," Lawrence said. "I know one thing: if I have a son, the first thing I am going to teach him is to make up his mind what he wants, regardless of his chances of ever having it. This idea of concentrating on the means and then looking around for the end—"

Hugh laughed. "I wouldn't worry about it too soon. There's many a slip, you know; you may still have time to think up something to buy with your million before you get it made. I'm going to teach my son to concentrate on the slip and then look around for the lip."

CHAPTER TWO

THE YEARS during which by Mrs. Middleton's reckoning Hugh's mother had been certain he was going to marry Anna had been a time of little certainty in other things at Nutwood. It had been the sort of time that gets spoken of in the plural and qualified as hard. There was even an autumn when the nuts had failed : a disaster of so dark a nature that it was hardly spoken of at all. Hugh was not told about it until afterward, nor Anna, since they were both away and did not have to see with their own eyes the ground covered with the green pecans, still tightly sealed in their unfinished husks, that had been stripped from the trees by a hurricane which was just enough of a hurricane to do that.

"What good would it do to tell them?" Lawrence said. "Hugh is working too hard already, and Anna—"

"I know," Mrs. Martin had agreed quickly. "We will just have to manage somehow."

Both Anna and Hugh were away so much during those years that managing without them came to be accepted as the natural thing to do. Mrs. Martin decided that whatever went on at home must be her problem and Lawrence's; at least for the present. Hugh in New Orleans, pursuing at rather long range whatever education he could keep in sight and still hold a job at Garibaldi's shipping office, and Anna at her finishing school in Mobile, were having their separate experiences and no doubt accumulating problems of their own. Mrs. Martin's idea where young people were concerned was to give them as much as possible the illusion of freedom while they forged their own chains. Poverty, being by nature opposed to this illusion, must be kept strictly in its place; and this, as she saw it, was at the moment between her and Lawrence.

Mrs. Middleton had known about the hurricane and could have guessed at some of the other blights that had fallen on Louisa's hopes. Being Louisa's oldest friend, she flattered herself she might even have divined the hopes; but she had been told almost as little as anybody about Louisa's actual plans for her three children, as she called them—and might as well call them, since Anna was sure to marry either Hugh or Lawrence in the end. And Anna did have money—which Louisa never would call anything. She wouldn't touch it with a ten-foot pole, even in conversation. She let Anna be educated out of it and dressed, but aside from that it existed for Louisa only as something to be accounted for on high. Anna's father had been her favorite cousin; she had come back from his funeral with Anna in her arms. That made three children and a sick husband—too sick even to have an opinion she could ask; not that it would have mattered, since there was nowhere else for the child to go. Anna was too young herself to care much where she was, and neither of the boys was old enough to mind her being there; they had no doubt accepted her at the age of four years exactly as they would have done at the age of four hours—as something provided by their mother without consulting them; whatever advantages she possessed over the newly born were probably lost on them. She might have been made interesting from a fairy-tale standpoint— as an orphan who would some day turn out to be a princess, or something of that nature, but any practical use they could have had for Anna must have been very small. Just when did a situation like that begin to change; and what did it change into? How had Louisa managed it? Or had she really managed it at all? Those were questions that might remain unanswered not only because Mrs. Middleton did not ask them but because Louisa didn't know.

For one thing, the changes that looked now so sweeping had seemed all so gradual at the time. The system of leaving everybody as free as possible—free even to change—had the advantage of greater freedom for Mrs. Martin too; it left her more time to think of other things—the things that had to be thought about—that were never free for anybody—and on the whole she couldn't see but what it worked as well as if she had worried more. It is true that her opportunity of seeing it in operation was much reduced after Hugh got his job in New Orleans and Anna began to be away at school; then the system could only be observed at close range during the holidays; but then there was an added pleasure in watching Anna and the two boys revert so naturally to their old footing. Mrs. Martin was surprised herself at the way they accepted without surprise the changes in each other, and the ease with which they conformed to the new situation. What was it Shakespeare said about not altering when you alteration found? In their case it seemed to her exactly what they ought to do. For instance, the kiss with which they met at first changing into the no-kiss of their later meetings without a sign on anybody's face—what could be nicer than that? And suppose she had tried to tell them what to do—how embarrassing it would have been for everybody!

The range of activity at Nutwood was immense. There was no illusion about the freedom with which they could all choose what they wanted to do, and whom they wanted to do it with— for there was a certain amount of sociability involved in most of the operations, even if one only chose a mule. Anything like conversation, however, was usually reserved for mealtimes or when it rained. Rain was about the only thing, except the night itself, that brought them in or even slowed them down. There was no winter. Anna looked back on the tennis court and the dancing class at Miss Delamere's academy as a bird might remember the perch and the swing it had left in its cage. The only useless exercise any of them ever indulged in at home was when they went rowing or swimming. The Sound was always Hugh's idea, and oftener than not he would be left to carry it out alone. More and more as they grew up, Anna and Lawrence would drop out and let him go by himself, or with the Coujac children—who were also growing up.

Hugh made no effort to conceal the way he felt about this. Being abandoned to a compelling joy is worse in some respects than being left alone with grief. It was in the hope of getting somebody—it might even be his mother—to come with him that he had bought the *Anita*—almost new and neither leaking nor smelling of fish.

"So that excuse doesn't hold any longer," he said. "I'm turning the *Sieve* over to John; I can go with him when I want to fish." *Sieve* was easier for the Coujacs to say than *Sylph,* and had long been more appropriate for the craft in question. "I can row you and Anna over to the Pass in your best bib and tucker now," Hugh told his mother; "or Lawrence can—or both of us, for that matter."

And that first summer they did go, in all those ways. That was the summer Hugh was nineteen.

There were four people in the Coujac family at that time; the two boys were still there and the younger of the two girls, whose mother had called her Olympe. She was called Olie now, and was to all intents and purposes a creature of the deep; so good in the water that it would have been unreasonable to think she could amount to much on land—if anybody had ever thought about it. Her short locks—slick when they were wet and rough when they were dry—were as little care to her as they would have been to a spaniel, and the bathing suits of odd shapes and sizes in which she usually appeared seemed to belong to her no more by the time she wore them out than they had when they were given to her—no more, one was tempted to think, than if they had been given to a fish.

"She is not as pretty as her sister was; how old is she now?" Mrs. Martin asked, one evening when they had been rowed over for a visit to Mrs. Middleton, and Olie had been on the beach to watch them embark. "Hugh told me you were coming," she said in her soft voice, helping them with their skirts. "We got her all ready; she's as dry as a bone."

"About my age, isn't she, Hugh?" Anna said.

"A little older, isn't she?" Hugh said. I doubt if Olie knows herself. I'm sure John doesn't."

"She must be about as old as Marie was when she went away," Mrs. Martin said. "Do they ever hear anything from her, Hugh? I mean do they ever say anything about how she's getting along?"

"She was married, the last thing they heard. Some dago with a fruit-stand, I believe."

"Good for her! Any kind of a stand sounds wonderful for that family," Mrs. Martin said. "Maybe she can take Olie now."

"Olie doesn't want to be taken," Hugh said. "Why should she? Olie is already a belle among the beachcombers."

"I can see how she would be," Mrs. Martin said. "A regular little siren."

"A short-haired Lorelei. I wonder how that idea of putting long hair on sea creatures ever got started," Lawrence said.

"I used to think Anna might do better if we cut hers off," Hugh said. They looked at Anna, eating her supper on the other side of the table, the light from the hanging lamp gilding her smooth head.

"I should think they all would," Lawrence said. "Where did it get started, Hugh?—the myth, I mean. Is it Northern or Southern? I'll bet whoever thought it up couldn't swim himself; some poet or other; poets can start anything."

"Yes, but what started the poet?" Hugh said. "It's like the chicken and the egg. Maybe seaweed had something to do with it." That wouldn't do for Anna, though; rushes maybe—tall grass—hand in hand with Plenty in the maize—Anna always started him; poetry, myth, religion even; either they had Anna in them or they didn't. What would he see in them if he didn't see

Anna? There had to be an image—He looked at her again. She had finished her lemon pie; she looked back at him and smiled.

The next summer Hugh was late in coming home. Professor Noel Middleton had offered him a job in the library at Tulane, cataloguing. Anna's vacation was already half over before his could begin, and even in what was still left of it she seemed to have left no place for him.

"She is having the most wonderful success with her new rose garden," his mother explained. "I started the cuttings for her in the winter, under glass, and some of them are blooming already. Did she show you?"

"I've already watered it for her twice," Hugh said. "It's wonderful. Does she ever sit down anywhere?"

His mother laughed. "Not very much, I'm afraid—not till we have a rain. It's been one of the longest dry spells in history. People in town don't notice it very much, but of course Lawrence has told you."

"It's dreadful," Hugh said. "Is there any water left in the Sound? How's the boat? I'll bet nobody has been in it since I was here at Easter."

"Not often, I'm afraid," Mrs. Martin said. "I see John Coujac occasionally, when he brings us fish. One of the boys has gone to Mexico, as something or other on a schooner. Why don't you go swimming this afternoon, Hugh, and see about the *Anita*? I suppose he's taking good care of her, but how do I know? And I want you to row me over to the Pass to attend to some business one day soon; some morning before it gets hot."

Many things that happened that summer came back to Hugh afterward on the names of roses—*Gloire de Dijon*—*Duchesse de Parme*. There were not many blooms so far in Anna's garden— only names; and Anna with her pots and watering-pots, and the dry days crackling underfoot and the sun blazing down overhead. He spent hours out there helping her in that raw-looking place that she kept telling him he wouldn't recognize the next time he came home. He toted water for her and mixed manure and got the bugs off, and tried not to look at her too much. She wore her hat out there—a wide straw hat a good deal the color of the rest of her; her eyes, drenched with sunlight, were just the color of the brim when she looked up at him. Straw-colored eyes. Nobody told the truth about things like that even when they saw it. That long level gaze that made the blood beat in his temples must not be straw-colored. Anna, Diana, who walked with death and morning on the silver horns, must not be out here mixing manure in the sun.

"Can't we go somewhere and cool off?" he asked her. "Let's take our supper over to the beach, and all come back by moon-light." The moons of a long dry spell were always enormous; he had noticed it ever since he could remember; he could have sworn they lasted longer too. His family made mighty little use of them, though. It would be just one more thing to do when they had already done too much. If they ate their supper on the beach it would only be for him, and God knows they had already done too much for him.

"You look thinner, Hugh," Mrs. Middleton told him. "Have you all been working too hard over there this summer?"

"I certainly haven't," he said. It was only the second time he had been to see Mrs. Middleton, and he would be going back to New Orleans next week. It had been a queer summer—what there was of it.

"Studying doesn't count, I suppose," Mrs. Middleton said. "I don't want Noel to keep hunting up extra work for you like this; I told him so the last time I saw him. Old Garibaldi is doing his best to kill you without Noel's help. *Il faut faire attention a ne pas gâter sa vie,* as my French grandmother used to tell us. What is Anna doing? *Toujours auprès de la rose?*"

"*Mais oui, madame.*" Hugh was sitting on the window-sill with the blue light from the Sound behind him. It was late afternoon, but still too warm to forsake the cool parlor for the porch.

"Of course at your age," Mrs. Middleton went on, "the idea of spoiling your life would never present itself; you can't imagine that enterprise failing, no matter what you do."

"Suppose we don't talk about me," Hugh said.

"Why not? You are a topic, aren't you?"

"A doubtful one. I've been doubtful in a good many directions lately; even my doubts are beginning to look doubtful to me. If I did spoil my life I wouldn't know what I was spoiling; and the life of a man who can't make up his mind about anything is not much worth saving, it seems to me."

He made this little speech with somber eyes, looking at her as if he thought that getting an answer might be doubtful too.

"Did you ever think," she asked him, "that indecision might be an indication of strength in a man, particularly a young man? It shows that he has more possibilities to choose from—or feels that he has. A weak man would be more afraid to try things, it seems to me."

"Suppose he had already tried a few and hadn't come off so well?" Hugh said.

"All the same, I can see how he might have run into graver temptations just because he had not been so quick to run away." She smiled. "That may be a dangerous opinion, Hugh; don't depend on it; and whatever you do, don't tell me anything you have been up to."

"Very well, I won't," he said. "I will only tell you that you have a wonderful opportunity to pray for me just now."

Late one afternoon in October, John Coujac came over, with no fish or other visible reason for coming, and asked to see Mrs. Martin.

"I think she's in the garden," Lawrence told him. "Here's John Coujac, Mamma," he called, leading the way to the gate.

Mrs. Martin, who was planting bulbs along the middle walk, rose from her knees and came to meet them, trowel in hand, glancing back as she did so at Anna in her rose garden. "Go hold the roses for her, Lawrence," she said. "Here, take the basket. Well, John."

With no fish, without even a hat to hold, there was nothing John Coujac could do with his hands but look at them hanging empty, while Mrs. Martin looked at him. "Is anything the matter?" she said.

"Jus' Olie," he said in his slow voice. "She wan' me to come. She t'ink she got a bébé now. She t'ink maybe you write to Hugh."

Mrs. Martin looked for something to sit down on, but there was nothing, so she stood without moving until John Coujac swam back into view, still looking at his hands and not at her. "Come with me to the house," she said gently; she seemed to feel sorry for him; just at the moment it was the only thing she seemed to feel at all.

"I suppose I shouldn't ask you, Lawrence, if you have any reason to believe it," she said when Anna had gone upstairs and she had laid John Coujac's errand before her younger son. "It could so easily be a lie. Only in that case," she went on when Lawrence did not answer, "I can't see why he came—why that poor silly girl would make him come—unless they expected to get something out of it. And even supposing it is true, which I simply can't believe, they still haven't said what they want me to do about it—except to write to Hugh."

"You don't think it could be just because she is fond of him—of Hugh I mean," Lawrence said, his color rising. "Wouldn't she want him to know, even without expecting him to do anything?"

His mother looked at him thoughtfully. "I simply don't know. It's hard to imagine people like the Coujacs, even when you've had them right under your eyes all your life. I wonder—" she hesitated. "Maybe you would write to him, son; don't you think it would be better for me to wait until—"

Until Hugh denied everything; Lawrence knew she wanted to say that. He wondered if she would still want to say it if everything were true.

Hugh's answer to his letter was prompt, and while as a declaration of innocence it fell short of Mrs. Martin's hopes, it was reassuring in some other ways. She may have seen in its phrasing another indication of heredity. Her father had been called upon to answer accusations in his day, not only with his tongue but with his pen, and while she had always assumed that the accusations were false, she knew his imperturbability had been famous.

It was not going to be his baby, Hugh's letter said—not in the sight of heaven, as Lawrence suggested, or in anybody's sight; certainly not in Olie's. Maybe his mother had better talk to Olie—"she wouldn't mind; she has no concealments to amount to anything and she is as far as possible from having any such motives as the ones you mention—or poor old John either. She made him come because she thought it might be one way to get me home—her idea of a siren song to lure me back to the ocean caves. But Olie is not going to worry; none of them are. And if only you, and especially Mamma, can just not do it either, I will be eternally grateful. I don't have to tell you—either of you—how sorry I am, both for the fool I've been and the trouble I have caused." Then, in a postscript: "Can you manage some way to keep Anna from finding out?"

He knew immediately, when he came home at Christmas, that they had not managed. He knew as soon as he looked at Anna—if he had been blind he thought he would still have known—that she had taken sides against him. Not Olie's side: a bigger side than that—the side of Woman. By the mystery of being a man he had been given the power to despoil this abstraction, and Anna saw him with strange eyes.

It was a miserable Christmas; and yet, with all the misery, he still had room to feel surprise. He could not have imagined Anna would take it like this. Dissapproval—condemnation even—was what he expected—something moral. This was physical.

"If somebody could talk to her!" He said that to himself a good many times as the holidays passed in an odd atmosphere of constraint that they all made a point of not noticing. He said it to Mrs. Middleton before he left. "My mother couldn't do it; it would seem too much like trying to patch me up," he told her; "you could, though."

"Thanks to my French grandmother, I suppose," Mrs. Middleton said. "She could always rush in where angels feared to tread. Do you know, Hugh, when I used to go home after a visit to my grandmother, it seemed to me I never heard anything interesting any more; nothing indiscreet; no personal questions—and personal answers too. Even now I often wonder why we have to be as dull as we are. The servants help a little of course—as much as we let them—or we would simply die of propriety. I suppose Anna learned about this Olie business from the servants. She doesn't go over there, does she—to the Coujacs, I mean?"

"Hardly ever. Anyhow, they didn't tell her. Olie is going to marry her Swede when his ship gets back. John told me that. I hope to goodness the baby has that color hair and eyes. On Anna's account."

"Tell me a little more about Anna—if you really want me to talk to her. Of course the thing that would help most would be for her to talk to me—if I knew any way to get her to do it. A girl is a complicated arrangement, Hugh; she has a whole set of emotions that are completely lacking in your make-up."

"I know that. Good Lord! Don't you suppose I have learned it by this time? All the same there is no point in her feeling the way she does—as if a thing like this had never happened in the world before. Anna is educated; she knows about the pagan gods—not to mention the Christian kings. A lot of high-class people have been known to behave this way, but she's got me down lower than an animal."

"Still, Hugh—you have to admit—"

"Of course I do; I'm not trying to excuse myself. I wouldn't blame Anna if she condemned me for a sinner, or despised me for a fool; but she doesn't; she just shrinks. That's what makes me sick."

Mrs. Middleton did not smile. She had not been told about the shrinking. Really, for a bright woman, Louisa Martin seemed to see less of what was going on—she sat over there in the woods with those three young people in positively explosive circumstances, and apparently as unconcerned as a hen on a nest full of eggs!

"Very well," she said, "I promise to do what I can. I'll talk to Anna and maybe to your mother too. I haven't seen as much of your dear mother lately as I should have done. She is a wonderful woman, Hugh." Mrs. Middleton was reflecting that her French grandmother might have found another epithet for Louisa.

The "circumstances" did not explode. In spite of Mrs. Martin's blindness or because of Mrs. Middleton's insight, or it may be for the simple reason that time unaided by anything is still the supreme diversion, it began to seem more and more probable as the months went by that these unorthodox developments would be kept strictly in their place—since they too had a place assigned to them. Even Olie, who was the element of least predictability, contributed a note of conformity in the end by providing herself with a husband and the baby with a name. The young seaman who backed this situation might be intermittent, but the name, which was Bjornsternborg, stood fast.

CHAPTER THREE

THE FOLLOWING SUMMER Anna, now seventeen and entirely finished by Miss Delamore, was invited by the parents of a classmate who wanted to carry the process further still in their daughter's case to go with them on the grand tour. This undertaking, whose grandeur usually began with a trip up the river on the *Kate Adams* to Chicago and ended with a voyage home by sea from New York, was far beyond anything Anna had ever dreamed of or even desired. "Still, it's exciting to be asked," she said.

Mrs. Martin looked at her thoughtfully. "You must go," she said, and went on to say that she knew Anna's father would have wished it—a finality always accepted at its face value by both of them.

What Anna's father would have wished was always entirely clear to Mrs. Martin and she had been from the first resolved on its fulfillment at whatever cost to herself. Anna must have every one of the things her father would have given her, even if she lost her in the process. Keeping her in the family was one thing and doing her duty by her was another. No dreams of hers must be allowed to get in the way of that. It was only by having this understanding with her conscience that Mrs. Martin had allowed herself to dream.

She had begun early. On that winter evening when she had come back from the funeral with Arthur Paget's sleepy little girl in her lap, she remembered thinking as the carriage turned in at the gate that it might be her daughter-in-law she was bringing home. And even then, in that first minute, she had tried not to ask herself *which one.* Having two sons for Anna to choose from, she could feel that she left her uncommitted—and her father would have wished that too. The grand tour would be the first long separation that had ever taken place between her and the boys. When she saw them again, it would be with eyes that had seen the world.

To Hugh, who met the steamer at New Orleans, it seemed at first that she had brought the world back with her. Anna, standing on the dock with skirts *à la polonaise,* fur at her throat, and a blue feather curled against her cheek, might have come from anywhere; she had the meaning of far cities; nothing seemed less likely than that she should be going home with him; her hand in its tight little glove did not feel as if it belonged to either one of them.

Sitting opposite to her on the train, trying to look at something else—to see the wonders she was telling him about instead of wondering at her—it struck him as a curious thing that he had noticed Anna's clothes so little in the past. As a rule, in other people, he noticed clothes a great deal; the idea that they were so much less important than behavior rather irritated him; they *were* behavior; dress was one of the rules of the game, and if the rules meant nothing, then what was the game? For some reason, though, he had never thought of Anna as trying to look one way rather than another; whatever happened when she put on a new dress had always seemed to happen to the dress and not to her.

This time it was different—the whole intention of it—and in some dimly analytical way he felt injured by it. She was asserting something new and mysterious; something she had learned: the queen's gambit.

"Hugh doesn't like me to be stylish," Anna said, taking off her hat before the mirror in Mrs. Martin's big downstairs bedroom and smiling at the three pairs of lighted eyes behind her. "I'm glad you and Lawrence do."

"She looks like that picture of the Princess Alexandra, don't you think so, Mamma?" Lawrence said.

"The dressmaker said I looked like Mrs. Langtry," Anna said, smoothing her smooth hair. "It will all be over tomorrow though. Wasn't it a shame for the train to be so late? I can hardly wait to see the garden."

"What makes you think Hugh doesn't like you this way?" Mrs. Martin asked her. "I would hate to think I had raised a boy like that."

"Because he scowled at me all the way on the train coming home," Anna said, looking at him in the glass. He was not scowling now.

"I must give her a party," Mrs. Middleton said. "I will do it right away, when Noel comes at Thangsgiving. We must all give her a party. Your mother mustn't let Anna settle back into that Maud Muller kind of life, Hugh. Anna has got to meet people; and by that I naturally mean men. I dare say she will marry you or Lawrence in the end, but she ought to have more to choose from in the beginning."

"Guess what she was choosing from last night," Hugh said— "she and Mamma and Lawrence, all sitting around the table with their seed catalogues, trying to decide which was the best cover-crop to plant over in the northwest field."

"Well—we can't have that, can we? Not at this juncture," Mrs. Middleton said.

Hugh looked thoughtful. "I don't believe agriculture taken seriously that way is becoming to a woman," he said presently. "Forcing things. The earth goddesses stood more for fulfillment; like your Maud Muller—raking the meadow sweet with hay; not planting it. Ruth didn't plant her alien corn either. You see them with their sheaves. Another power has to be invoked to do the sowing—" His eyes were far away. Poetic truth was wonderful; it ran so true. Even if the form had changed, the meaning would be the same. There was an unbroken austerity about it; a sort of last judgment—

Mrs. Middleton did not make her usual effort to follow the thoughts that darkened his face. "Still," she said, "you can't blame Anna for wanting to be something more than symbolic about her farming. Imagine how it would hamper her to have to stay in the picture all the time! Did you ever think how it would hamper a man to run his business from that kind of a standpoint? It's too bad men and women have to go on making such an effort to please each other, since that is really the thing they are trying to do. You would think by this time they would have got the hang of it better. Do you ever wonder what you might be expected to symbolize?"

He shrugged his shoulders. "What's the use? I walked out of Anna's picture gallery some time back."

"Just two years ago, wasn't it?" Mrs. Middleton looked at him reflectively. "I saw Olie the other day," she said; "over there on the beach playing with the baby. He really is cunning. I stopped the carriage and called them up to the road to give them some candy I had bought at Gulfport. He's the spittin' image of Olie— he looks like a little sea-urchin or something; when she put him down on the sand he actually started crawling backwards, like a crab. I don't see a trace of Bjorn in that baby—nor of any other man on shore. My own theory leans to a merman—a Forsaken Merman, like Matthew Arnold's poem—

She steals to the window, and looks at the sand;
And over the sand at the sea—"

Hugh did not say anything. He was not sitting in the window this time; they were at the other end of the room, where a fire was burning on the hearth, so he looked at the fire.

"I am going to ask you something, Hugh," Mrs. Middleton said after a while. "Don't answer if you don't want to. Does Anna have any idea how you feel about her?"

"Does anybody?"

"Do you?" she said.

The winter was very gay indeed, in Anna's honor and in honor of the tradition that prevails in small sociable places, where the same things can be done any number of times by the same people without losing any of their original intention. From Thanksgiving until Mardi Gras, Anna went on meeting people, which even if it did mean meeting men, could under the circumstances only mean meeting them over again; so that whatever choice was offered her among them must have been numerically small. At all events the arrival of Lent found her still at Nutwood without having chosen, so far as could be guessed, anything that was likely to take her away from there.

Hugh was at home now more than he had been for the last four or five years and had taken over whatever part of the work Lawrence would resign to him—for the present, Lawrence said. In one way or another, it seemed to Hugh, they all said that—or meant it. Only about him; never about themselves; not even about Anna. They were supposed to be permanent; they would be there forever, stepping out with the seasons, while he skulked around for the present.

"How long is the present?" he asked Lawrence. "What is it you are expecting me to do when it is all used up? Where do I go then?"

Lawrence laughed. "Isn't that for you to decide? The present is while you are deciding. If it is anything like writing, though, I don't see why you can't stay right where you are and do it. Of course Mamma has all sorts of ideas about politics. I tell her that's a different game these days from the one her father played in, but she seems to think it is only waiting for you to come along and straighten it out; she thinks it is only rotten for the present."

So that was the outlook: he was to be a writer; a poet probably—a follower of the muses and the long-bowed Apollo. And if not that, then a politician of some kind; a statesman, his mother called it. In either case he was to have as little to do as possible with nature—as they called that. While they marched hand in hand with universal law, he was to be side-stepping the procession—doing his own little dance. It ought to be a wonderful feeling—to see life stretching ahead of you the way they saw it, without a break, knowing every day exactly what was expected of you. All the same, there was less tranquillity about it than you would imagine—and less time; the days just simply disappeared as far as you were concerned; you would never know they had been there from any feeling they gave you; you had to go look at something like potatoes, or corn, that you had planted. It was all right, of course, to turn your personal record over to a field of something, but there ought to be more tranquillity for you, even if there had to be less for nature. His mother never sat down unless she was peeling something, and Lawrence, as far as he could see, never opened a book any more.

And Anna—there was no use looking for anything in Anna that you wouldn't find in Tempe or the dales of Arcady. She was more mythological than ever. The way she gave in to the elements! It was like something in *The Golden Bough.* The spring was like the embrace of love to her; it made him think of Danaë, of Leda; it made him wonder what was going on. Weather seemed to mean as much to Anna as it did to vegetation; he had watched her out in the rain, wet all over like a tree, and apparently with no more idea of coming in than the tree had. "Listen—" she said serenely one day when the lightning struck something so close it made him fairly jump out of his skin. Well, he hoped he hadn't lived through a winter like the last one—Mrs. Middleton's idea of a winter—to start being jealous of Olympian Jove.

He wrote a good deal of poetry that spring—not with any idea of publishing it; for the present too; and once in a while he gave Anna some of it to read. Not because he expected her to like it; because he couldn't help it, probably—

Wind drifting on a sandy place,
Day after day, grain after grain,
Might through the years
Carve on the desert's face your face—
A forehead with no path for pain,
Eyes with no wells for tears.

Modeling not meant for those
Mortal intaglios
Cut in our clay;
Here no lighted moment goes,
No shadows stay;
No joy, no grief
Shall lift this low relief.

How should I please
With brief idolatries
An endless effigy?
How should my ardors urge,
My dreams beguile,
An image that may not emerge
To weep or smile
Or while away eternity
A little while?

He watched her read it, taking her time about it; she read it more than once. "It's lovely," she said handing it back to him. "It's a new meter, isn't it?"

"No," he said.

"Well, anyhow it's lovely," she repeated.

"Do you know what it's about?"

"Isn't it a sort of fable—a man in love with a woman who hasn't any heart, or any soul—"

"Or any sense? Then why is he in love with her?"

"Her looks, I reckon—the way she looks to him. Isn't it a little like Pygmalion and Galatea?"

"Very good," he said, taking it back. "Little Anna gets an A on that."

"A for Anna was what you always said. We haven't either of us changed much, have we?" she smiled, searching his face for what he used to be. With those eyes. A for adoration—A for ass—

It was at the end of this summer—Anna's idea of a summer—that he made up his mind to try for the desk on the *Richmond Democrat*.

The idea met with general encouragement. His mother took it as at least a step in the right direction—a public step. Lawrence seemed to think any direction he chose would be right for him, and Anna did not seem to think. Which was quite as it should be, Mrs. Middleton told him. Anna would do her thinking when he was no longer there.

"If she went on having you and Lawrence both there all the time, I really don't believe she would ever manage to fall in love with either one of you," Mrs. Middleton said. "That composite situation would never strike a girl as being anything but safe and comfortable and the very opposite of romantic."

Hugh looked at her with interest; this was a view of the matter that he had altogether missed. "You mean—" he said, and waited; her meanings were better when nobody helped her with them.

"I mean it would never occur to Anna that you and Lawrence could start being rival brothers and behaving the way they do in books—hating each other, and pretending to be each other—and pouring poison in each other's ears. I must say I can't imagine it myself, but I can get scared enough without that."

"Scared of what?"

"Oh, complications—somebody getting hurt. I can get scared over you whether you go or stay, if you keep on the way you are now."

"Keep on where—as I am now? And what am I now, if you don't mind? Don't say a poet."

She looked at him thoughtfully. "I will say a lover by the grace of God; one of the few I have known in the course of my life. That is why I feel favorably disposed toward you, Hugh : you are unusual.

He did not say anything.

"And that being the case," she went on, "I would like to give you some unusual advice; only I don't believe there is any. We might as well consult the tea-grounds—" she held out her hand for his cup.

"No, tell me," he said—"tell me what you think I ought to do. About Anna—about all of them there at home; about going or staying—about living or dying, for that matter." He handed her his cup.

"Well, of course," she said as she filled it, "I always have to remind myself that you are very young so far—don't burn yourself!"

He already had, and did so again immediately in repudiation of everything her words implied. He didn't want to go into that youth business again—reminding her that a man's age counted for no more in the balance of his achievement than his inches did. *How tall was Alexander, Pa, that people called him great*—how old was Robespierre, or Byron, or a lot of others that he hoped he did not resemble in anything except the accident of youth?

"Very well, then," he said; "tell me anything that you think suited to my tender years."

She considered this a little. "The brother going out into the world to seek his fortune ought to have an understanding with the lady before he starts, oughtn't he?"

"You mean I ought not go to Richmond without asking Anna to marry me? She would think I was crazy; I would be crazy."

Mrs. Middleton laughed. "Suppose you don't ask her anything; suppose you just tell her a few things—not too many; don't frighten her. Anna probably has no idea you are in love with her."

"Then she is crazy."

"Have you ever told her? In so many words, I mean; not poetry; she thinks you write poetry because you are a poet; anything back of that would seem to her immaterial. And will you be able to write letters to her, by the way? To her—not to the family."

He shook his head. " 'What does Hugh say?' They would be sure to ask her that."

"So much the more reason, then, for the understanding. Whatever Hugh says will have a different meaning to her after that."

So it was all a matter of words; written, spoken—Sing, O Goddess—To write the *Iliad* or to make a living on the newspaper or to say things that would have a different meaning to Anna—it was all a matter of words.

On an afternoon a few days after this conversation he had gone to the Pass on an errand for his mother, and Anna had gone with him. It was his last evening at home, and so as a special act of grace she had consented to go in the boat instead of the buggy, and they were walking back through the wood.

The expedition had been attended by no jarring circumstance of any kind. They had embarked in the *Anita* and disembarked without hail or farewell from any of the Coujacs, who seemed none of them to be at home. Out on the water, skirting the edge of a low-lying island, they had seen what they took to be the *Sylph*, mended now by the industry of Bjorn and rigged with a sail. It was too far to see if Olie was on board; much too far to see the baby.

It was a lovely evening after the manner of Wordsworth—calm and fair and quiet as a nun. The sky over the water was still pink with sunset, but the wood held only shadows. "You are like a white moth flitting among the trees, in that dress," Hugh said. "You are the only lighted thing in sight. Better jump this—" It had rained the night before and the little stream that crossed the path was full; the logs laid in it to step on looked wet and slippery. He had cleared them as he spoke and now held his hand back to Anna, who obediently gathered up her skirts and jumped. He did not let go her hand; instead, he drew her closer. "Come to me, Anna; look at me," he said. "Have you forgotten that I used to kiss you?"

The voice with which his grandfather had "swayed thousands" was now attuned to meet the ear of one lone maiden in a wood—one altogether unprepared for what had happened to it, or to the eyes now looking into hers. The hand he was holding began to tremble; she looked at the path beyond him as if she meant to fly.

He let go her hand. "What is the matter? What do you think I want to do to you, Anna?" he said. "Can't I make a fool of myself without scaring you to death?" Blackness had descended on him; the music was dead.

"Don't frighten her," Mrs. Middleton had said. Were girls supposed to be frightened if a man made love to them—girls like Anna? Or was it being in the woods this way—in the evening? Or was it going in the boat—He remembered suddenly about Olie; that must be it; poor little Olie out there contaminating the Gulf of Mexico.

Anna was walking ahead now and he followed her in silence. This time tomorrow, thank God, he would not be here. The country was too much for him anyhow; the quiet country; nature. Even without Anna in it nature never gave him any peace. The mean city was what he needed; the ugly streets; a dirty newspaper office—the kind of place where nothing would have to stir in him but his soul.

CHAPTER FOUR

THIS OUTLINE of Grub Street, though Hugh had drawn it more from books than from anything he knew of Richmond, where he had never been, turned out to be in some respects a fairly accurate picture of the setting in which he found himself when he took up his duties on the *Democrat.* Certainly the room he shared with Jackson—its bare boards and grimy windows, its wastebaskets and spittoons—was everything he could have meant by dirty newspaper office. It was, however, the last place where, had he known Jackson, he would have thought of introducing his soul, even as a private conception of his own. Jackson would have wanted to know what he meant by it; he would have made him define it; he wouldn't have let up on it until it exploded in his face. It took Hugh only a few days to learn that most of the definitions in any bright lexicon he had hitherto possessed could be counted on to arouse in Jackson a bullying attitude, not only toward the term in question but toward language in general.

"You seem to think there is something ordained about a dictionary," Jackson said. "You talk as if it had come down from Sinai."

Hugh wondered if Jackson's contempt for the tools of his trade had been bred by the astonishing familiarity with which he seemed to handle them. He could never get used to the change that came over him the minute he took up his pen. It was as if he were caressing something—something soft and pliable; like stroking a cat. The pages slipped from under his hand and fell without spot or blemish into the printer's basket beside him.

Nothing sputtered, nothing scratched. It did not seem fair, somehow, for him to find words so docile when he gave them so little
faith.

"You talk as if they were something outside of you," Jackson
said—"something in themselves, going on independently of the
sounds you have learned to make with your mouth. I know one
thing: whatever is going on outside of you, it isn't words."

"*In the beginning—*" Hugh began.

"*Was the Word.* The beginning of what? The beginning
of trouble, if you ask me," Jackson said. " 'Now that we can
communicate, you shut up'—that was probably the opening
sentence."

Hugh laughed. "You know, that's funny, Jackson," he said.
"Is it original?"

"Of course it ain't. How could anything be original, dressed
up in those old rags?"

It was a good thing, Hugh thought, that the theme was so
entertaining, since there seemed no prospect of its ending. How,
when he came to think about it, could it end? Jackson's side of it
being directed against all the verbal noises hitherto invented, he
would have to resort to an inchoate bellow of some sort before he
could prove his point.

"Maybe so," Jackson said; "but wouldn't it be a good idea to
sound like what you really are—the way a bull does, or a frog—
instead of trying to sound like something you never even saw—
some abstraction or other? Truth—virtue—a man will even talk
about the virtue of an animal; a horse, for instance. Imagine the
horse talking about it!"

Hugh thought this over. "Don't you think," he suggested,
"that maybe the horse has the advantage of us in not having
to promise anything? We have a lot of traffic with the future;
we need words for that; they are a sort of pledge, aren't they—a
promise to pay?"

"Keeping your word. Sounds like something, doesn't it?"

"It is something. At least until you have kept it, it is," Hugh said. "Don't forget about the man who

> —*had two witnesses to swear*
> *He kept it once in Berkeley Square.*"

Jackson snorted. He turned in his swivel chair, plunged his pen into the inkwell, and the singular silence that follows on an uproar took possession of the room.

When Hugh went home in September he had been away almost a year; the longest absence of his life, and the first one that had impressed him as being something in itself and not just an empty space between two realities. Time had not merely lapsed, it had been busy while he was away, changing the old dimensions, setting the new signs. Unfamiliarity began as soon as he got within the radius of the familiar.—So this was how it looked, he kept thinking.

The train was late, as he knew it would be. He had written them to leave the *Anita* tied up at the dock near the station, instead of sending something to meet him that would mind waiting, like a horse and buggy; his baggage could be met later—whenever it suited the horse; and, sure enough, there the *Anita* was.—So this was how she looked.

He threw in his handbag, untied the rope, and took up the oars. It was the meeting he had counted on, and not too late after all; the evening was still bright. The sky and the water embraced him in an equal rose. Almost an equal stillness too. He could see, however, by the unkempt appearance of the beach as he rowed on, that there had been a storm; the familiar evidence of shells and seaweed littered the sand, with now and then a piece of timber washed ashore, or a green branch from a tree. If he had come yesterday or the day before, it would have been the buggy after all.

There was a lot of rubbish in front of John Coujac's house; he thought for a moment, as he turned the boat in to shore, that the roof must have blown off; then he saw it was only the dock that had washed up on the beach. The poor old *Sylph* had been dragged up out of harm's way and lay in a capsized position among the boards. Somebody was sitting on her—it was Anna. This was the meeting he had not counted on; not even in a dream.

She came toward him as he jumped out and pulled the *Anita* up after him. "You've had a blow, I see," he called to her. "How do you happen to be here? Where is everybody?"

"Cousin Louisa came too," she said, giving him her hand. "But you were so late; she went back to get the buggy and drive to the station. I told her I would wait a little longer; I was about to go, but just then I saw you coming."

She had taken her hand back, but he held her eyes. "When was the storm?" he said. "Let's sit here where you were. Was it very sudden? This old tub looks as if she must have been out in it; she seems to have lost her rigging. None of the crew lost, I hope. Anna—what has happened? Was anybody drowned?"

"The baby," she said. She sat down again on the boat and looked up at him standing beside her. "Olie had taken him out with her—over by the island."

"But how on earth, Anna—"

"It was so sudden, Hugh. She didn't have time to do anything—she was trying to take down the sail."

"But couldn't she swim with him? Couldn't she grab one of the oars or something?"

"She couldn't find him. She tried for hours, out there all by herself. The boat blew in and John thought they were both lost. But even when he went out after her he could hardly make her come. And all that night, he said, she kept going down on the beach and listening for him. Oh, the poor little thing, Hugh—the poor little thing!"

"Don't cry, Anna," he said, sitting down by her and taking her cold hands. "Where are they now—the Coujacs? Is anybody there—in the house, I mean?"

She shook her head. "They are at the funeral. They found the baby yesterday, washed up on the island." She turned to him, her tears streaming. Her hat had fallen off and lay on the sand at her feet. "Oh, Hugh," she sobbed, burying her face against his shoulder, "I didn't know anything could be as sad as that."

"Don't cry, Anna," he said again, his arm around her, his lips touching her hair. "Oh, my love, my love, don't cry!"

"We must go," she said, drawing a deep breath and lifting her face.

Hugh picked up her hat and held it while they stood together looking at the sea.

"I keep wondering how Olie can bear to look at it—and listen to it," Anna said. "It seems to me she would want to go away somewhere where there isn't any water."

"She won't, though; she'll be out on it again tomorrow maybe, in this same old boat. You can't hold anything against the sea; it is too much like God for that. *Though He slay me, yet will I trust Him.*"

"Not the sea, Hugh—how can you trust the sea?"

"You can't trust it not to kill you, if that's what you mean. You can't trust God not to do it either. It is love you are trusting, Anna; your own love; the love you really know about."

They walked home hand in hand, back into their childhood. So this was how it felt when innocence and peace belonged to him and did not have to be bought with a miracle; the miracle of sacrifice and of forgiveness.

"But Anna was already different, Hugh," Mrs. Middleton told him. "She was different before this happened; I have been noticing it all summer. I have seen a good deal more of Anna lately; she likes me better than she used to. By that I mean she likes to listen to me, which is all I have to go by these days; all the other signs have failed."

"And what does she hear when she listens? What is the formula?"

"Does it matter—if it works?"

"Then, if it was you—" Hugh began, but she interrupted him.

"I don't mean that; it would have taken years for me to talk Anna into feeling the way she has since this tragedy; but I did do something for her imagination. She had actually been going over to the beach sometimes; I saw her once or twice sitting on the sand with Olie and the baby, and after that, of course, I felt free to mention them whenever I needed to. It helped a lot for the baby to be so cunning; nobody could deny him his right to be here—poor little sea-urchin!"

Hugh, sitting on the window-sill, looked out at the sea.

"And now," Mrs. Middleton began again, "the main thing is you."

He turned back into the room. "You mean I have got to change too?" he said.

"Not in the way you feel; you feel exactly to suit me; I've told you that; it's your technique you have got to look out for. You have simply got to go slow, Hugh, even if it is the one thing you can't do. You have got to manage not to give Anna so much more than she is ready for."

"But I do go slow," he protested. "You have no idea! I never touch her; only that one time, there on the beach that first day, when she was crying; not even when she hands me something at the table; I nearly dropped the butter-dish trying not to."

Mrs. Middleton laughed. "Don't be ridiculous, Hugh. Anna isn't going to notice touches; she is not going to misconstrue things."

"Or construe them either? You think I can look at her, then— I mean all I want to? I have been trying not even to do that—not below her chin at any rate."

She laughed again. "You don't notice her new dresses?"

"How can I, when she shines through them like a lamp? She always has. Anna has the kind of body that could go straight into heaven without being changed at all. I have thought that lots of times."

"And said it too, I suppose?"

He looked darkly at the floor.

"Why must you, Hugh? That's exactly the kind of thing I mean. Why can't you talk to Anna about something like her soul?"

"And say what—separate from the rest of her? Let's hear you say something about Anna's soul! How do you know she's got one? Anyhow, love doesn't take people apart like that. The thing I like the best about it is the way it helps you to hold things together."

"But a poet, Hugh—you are supposed to be a poet. Look at Shakespeare—look at Donne: the way they took the ladies apart. A poet can write a sonnet to his mistress's eyebrow."

"Exactly: and there you have his mistress. That is, if he's a poet you do; of course if he only thinks he's one, you only have him."

The days of this September, long as they still were and lighted by an indefatigable sun, were none the less, like the days of all the vacations Hugh remembered, not long enough for his family to get through with what they had to do by daylight, nor when darkness supervened, to get through talking about it. In the sweat of thy brow shalt thou eat bread. Did the Lord God know it would turn out to be so interesting? As far as he could see, Adam's curse was every bit as exciting as the stock market. Why was it always considered virtuous to make money agriculturally? People seemed to be born with the conviction that farming was what they were intended to do; even when they did it badly; even if they overdid it and turned it into a sort of debauch. And women seemed to be even worse than men, once they got started. This time it was not roses: it was hundreds of little cabbage plants. Anna had gone in for winter vegetables.

"She is really doing it scientifically," his mother explained. "It seems to fascinate her even more than flowers. It is really wonderful to see how absorbed she is in it."

"I don't think it's wonderful," Hugh said. "Or maybe I've just got used to it. Anna's always absorbed, as you call it."

Mrs. Martin looked up from the peaches she was peeling. "You mean you think it isn't good for her—to be so interested in what she's doing—or that she ought to be doing something else?"

"Oh, I'm not criticizing; I just can't seem to think it's wonderful for anybody to do exactly what they want to do, regardless of what they pay for it. It seems to me what Anna is paying is about all of those 'advantages' you were so careful to see she didn't miss getting. She could do what she is doing now without having been to school at all. You aren't afraid she might forget how to read, are you?"

Mrs. Martin laughed. "I hadn't thought of that," she said; "but naturally I don't expect her to go on this way. Right now, though—" She hesitated. "You see, Hugh, with you away like this—"

"I reckon you don't expect me to go on being away either, do you, Mamma? I believe Lawrence is the only one of us you feel permanent about, isn't he?" Hugh was smiling, but she did not answer with a smile.

"All the same, Hugh," she said presently, "while you *are* here, I wish you would tell us more about your work—about your writing, I mean, and about the paper. It would be good for all three of us to put our minds on something not quite so—well, say practical—for a change. We certainly don't want Anna to forget how to read. Not if you are going to be a famous writer. And that is one thing I *do* expect." She was smiling now, giving his shoulder an affectionate pat as she went out with the pan of peaches.

What else did she expect? What had she stopped expecting? The difference in Anna—had she expected that—or had she wanted Anna to be different? Love holds things together, he had told Mrs. Middleton. His mother probably believed that too; she was holding this thing together—believing that she could—by giving all her love to it; trying to give it equally to them all.

He had found the old hammock up in the hot lumber room under the mansard, and hung it in its old place between two of the big pecan trees. The shaggy bark had almost closed over the rings; he had to cut it away before the rope could pass through them. "Come lie down and cool off," he called to Anna, catching her on her way from the garden to the house.

"And let you swing me to sleep the way you used to?" she asked, coming toward him across the grass.

"Can you listen in your sleep? Do you realize how little time I have had to talk to you since I have been here?"

"Don't swing me, then," she said, sitting down in the hammock and taking off her hat. "Too high—I can barely touch. But isn't it heavenly and cool! I had forgotten what it was like." She looked up into the branches and then down at him. One of the differences in her was the way she looked at him.

Hugh moved his chair so he could sit facing her. "The days are running out, Anna; only five more."

"Cousin Louisa thinks we ought to make you tell us more about your work—I mean the things you write for the paper," she said, keeping her lovely eyes on his face. "She wants you to read us the ones you have with you—if you still have time."

"I haven't," he said. "I haven't time to read you anything. I want to talk to you—out loud; not just to myself the way I have to do up there in Richmond. I want to call you by all your names that begin in A for Anna—Artemis, Astarte, Aphrodite—

Saw the white implacable Aphrodite,
Saw the hair unbound and the feet unsandalled—"

He looked at her unruffled head and down at her dusty little shoes. "I don't want to go away," he said in a lost voice.

She held the hammock still, her toes touching the grass, listening.

"It is exactly like dying, to go away," he said. "Every day that I can't see you is just a day of blindness for me, Anna; and yet when I am here—you see how it is! Why can't you stay with me—why can't you talk to me more?" He looked at her imploringly.

"But I do; I love to talk to you," she said. "Only there seems to be so much to do, and talking does take time, Hugh."

"I want it to take time," he said. "I want it to take eternity. God has got to give me back every minute I have to spend away from you. That is the bargain I have made with Him—up there in Richmond, and even down here—even ten minutes from now when you jump up and say you have got to go water something. How am I ever going to learn all the things I have got to know about you, the way we are now—always being separated and having to start over? And even when I am with you and have you right under my eyes you are changing every minute."

Right under his eyes she was changing now. She put her hand up to her throat; her color drained away.

"But people are not supposed to know each other like that, Hugh," she said in a low voice. "They can't; they shouldn't even want to."

"But they do want to; I do. I want to know every time your heart beats—every time you draw your breath. Can't you understand, Anna? You say people should not be like that, but love *is* like that; it is the only way it can be. Why won't you let me tell you? Some day you will have to know. Sit down again and listen; I know you are busy, but please, Anna—" He put out his hand to stop her, then let it fall. What was the use? She went up the steps and into the hall without looking back.

"I suppose now she would like to turn me into a stag or something," he thought bitterly. "Anna wants to be as private all the time as if she were taking a bath."

He turned back to the empty hammock and presently lay down in it. *Casta Diva*—chastity—modesty—he believed it was just plain exclusiveness. Anna wasn't what people meant by modest—whatever they did mean. At any rate she didn't get embarrassed the way girls were supposed to do. His mother and even Lawrence talked about things before Anna that he would never mention before any girl alive. That sort of modesty didn't go with farming. Adam's curse. Eve's curse—maybe it didn't go with that either; in the line of nature; if you didn't stop to think about it. He believed Anna would be perfectly capable of marrying a man and having a houseful of children without knowing anything about love—God's curse.

"I don't seem to have made any progress," he told Mrs. Middleton when he stopped to say good-by to her on his way to the station. "She isn't holding Olie against me any more—it isn't that. She probably realizes by this time that there wasn't as much excitement over that episode as she imagined, either in heaven or hell. It isn't me she's afraid of; it's love; she can't stand the idea of giving up; of losing any part of herself—her integrity. She thinks there is something weak about letting go. I can't make her see that holding on to things is not the idea—that it is opposed to the very nature of love. Losing her life to find it—that little rudiment is where she sticks. I don't believe Anna is even a Christian. Maybe she doesn't have to be; maybe she is just immortal."

"Well, in that case you certainly don't have to hurry her, do you?" Mrs. Middleton said. "You can't get married yet awhile anyhow, so you are not obliged to teach her everything at once. It is probably a very good thing for you to be going away again just at this stage of her education. You've given her plenty to think about, Hugh; she will probably just about have time to absorb it between now and Christmas.—It is Christmas, isn't it, this time?"

"If they don't keep shoving more work on me."

"Well, that's a good thing too; you know it is. And, by the way, I wish you would leave me that paper if you don't mind. I'm really interested in your old *Democrat*. I had no idea any newspaper these days—not even the one you were on—would sponsor a real literary controversy. Don't you feel flattered with all those letters coming in?"

"All abusing me? I may lose my job."

"If you do, you will have plenty of others offered to you. But that is what I like about your paper; publishing the letters that way. It reminds me of Byron and his *English Bards*. Such a relief from politics."

"It will be politics before we get through with it. You watch," Hugh said.

Looking at the clock after he had gone, Mrs. Middleton was afraid he had missed his train. Would she ever reach the point where she did not feel obliged to make a man miss his train? Even a boy like Hugh—even Noel.

Missing the Yazoo Valley, however, was not always an easy thing to do. Hugh found when he got to the station that he had not minutes but hours on his hands before there was any prospect of his train's departure. He would go back to Mrs. Middleton's, he decided; he had left the boat tied up at the station landing; or—he looked at his watch—there might even be time to go home. The picture that rose before him of the place, the hour, as they were now, and he not in them, made him feel suddenly as if he were not anywhere. He knew what they would all be doing, what they did every evening at just this time; the only difference was his not being there, and that seemed all at once to be the difference between life and death.

It was absurd, of course; it had exactly the same absurdity and the same intensity as a dream—to be rowing back like this instead of being already miles away in the opposite direction. He seemed to have turned back the course of something. And at home they would expect to see him as little, after these few hours, as if he had crossed the Styx; which was only to say that they would not be expecting him at all. Well, at least he hoped he would not be invisible.

Eva, who was washing the supper dishes in the kitchen when he came in, not only saw him but saw him without surprise. His mother was at the spring-house, skimming up, she told him. "I don't know 'zactly where the others is. You missed your train didn't you, Mr. Hugh?"

"Just late," he said; "three hours late. You'll fix me some supper, won't you, Eva?"

He turned down toward the spring-house, where the milk was kept. The others would be in the garden. He did not see them as he passed, but he did not have to. Anna would be sprinkling, Lawrence filling cans from the rain barrels by the shed. He could hear them talking—nice cheerful conversation suitable for the ears of young cabbages.

"One more?" Lawrence asked.

"I don't believe so," Anna said. "Don't they look flourishing? Now if we could only have a good rain—"

He went on to the spring-house. They would still be there when he came back, gloating over their handiwork; feeling the same about the same things, the growing things. And the evening and the morning were the third day.

CHAPTER FIVE

THERE WAS NO DOUBT about its being a good thing for Hugh to have more space given him on the paper; it would have been better, however, if the almost deplorable ease with which he filled it had been balanced by a closer acquaintance with the local matters he was now and then expected to comment upon. Left to himself, his inclination when he took up his pen was to listen to almost any voices rather than the regionally insistent, and a certain amount of such irrelevance had proved acceptable to the readers of the *Democrat,* who had no objection to being pulled up a bit. They did not want to be pulled up into the clouds, however, and on no account did they want to be left dangling. They expected to be let down neatly at the end and landed well within the policy of the paper, and that was an ambiguous region where even after all these months Hugh still found it easy to confuse the landmarks and mistake the boundaries.

"Been expressing your ideas ever since you were born, haven't you? Never had anybody to stop you," Jackson said.

"What's the matter this time?" Hugh asked him.

"Just what do you mean by 'disestablished intellect'?"

"Just what you think I mean, I expect."

Jackson snorted. "I suppose you call yourself a democrat," he pursued.

"I suppose I'd better, seeing where I work."

"You're a high Tory in your taste, wherever you work," Jackson said. "Maybe you're more advanced in other directions; maybe you keep all your superstitions for your æsthetic side."

Advancement was one of the things the policy called for; advancement on all fronts and in the biggest kind of a hurry; not any slow march of the élite, the chosen.

"And why did you have to go bring in Aristotle?" Jackson groaned. "You can't ever go around beating the bush with Aristotle and not start some hare or other who thinks you mean him."

"I did," Hugh said.

"And then you ask me what's the matter! You knew he was bound to come back at you, didn't you? A certain amount of controversy on a dull subject like literature is all right—it sort of wakes up the old alumni; but you don't have to pick out the poet laureate of Virginia to try your standards on."

"Does he call himself that?" Hugh said. "Good Lord!"

"He lets his friends do it; he's got plenty of 'em, too. How do you think they are going to like what you call him—let Aristotle call him—the *Democrat* call him?"

It seemed that poetry in the columns of the *Democrat* was not to be considered apart from the poet. The policy called for that too.

Nor was there any reason that Jackson could see why Hugh should be considered apart from his prose, either by those who read it or by those who paid him to write it. "And if I was you I wouldn't use up too much of it on Marshall Wise Carter. He may or may not be the poet laureate of Virginia, but there are two or three other things he is that are more important than that in an election year. How do you think it looks for you to come out and insinuate that the man we've got up for governor has got a son that can't write poetry? Tryin' to split the party wide open!"

When Jackson talked like that he generally found Hugh ready to be admonished as well as to laugh, and on this occasion he found him entirely willing to end the controversy that had reminded Mrs. Middleton of Byron, as Byron never ended anything—by simply dropping the subject. He did not propose to eat his words, however, or to let the *Democrat* eat them. Just so the policy did not call for a recantation. He did not believe even Mr. Carter would like that.

His acquaintance with Mr. Carter had been too impersonal for him to give much thought to any likes and dislikes of a personal nature he might all the time have been entertaining behind either the literary or the political front. It came as a surprise to him—it was even a surprise to Jackson—to learn that what the poet laureate wanted was not an apology but a fight. He had, it seemed, already passed out of earshot of any palinode his critics might be induced to sing.

Hugh had heard it said that a man who intended to insult somebody had better pick out any state in the Union to do it in rather than Virginia; it now occurred to him that care in picking out the insult might also be advisable. It would seem that in this particular case he had hit on not only the worst locality but the worst affront. Not that Mr. Carter ever came out and said so—or even let his friends do it. Nobody mentioned poetry any more; the issue was by this time altogether submerged in the verbal fog of an election year. It was clear, however—Jackson said it was clear—that nobody was to be placated with the pen. The fact that weapons of a greater precision were still more favored in Virginia than elsewhere was one of the things that made argument in that state a greater risk.

"The best thing to do," Jackson said, "is just not to do anything. It's too close to Christmas for that sort of foolishness anyhow. Let him go home and talk to Santa Claus. You're getting off pretty soon yourself, aren't you?"

It was precisely his preoccupation with his chances of getting off that kept Hugh from weighing these presumably less immediate matters with as much attention as he might otherwise have given them. He simply could not give a thought to anything that might happen when he got back after Christmas. The idea of being expected to stand up and try to kill Mr. Carter—or even try not to kill him—for nothing but writing the kind of poetry he did would no doubt seem just as ridiculous to him after Christmas as it did now; but now at least he did not have to think of it—all sorts of things could happen between now and then.

In this way Hugh found himself poorly prepared to answer the formal requirements presented to him only a few days before the date set for his departure, by the young man who waited upon him with the challenge. The two ideas uppermost in his mind seemed equally impossible to bring forward. He could not tell Mr. Carter's second that he didn't want to fight anybody until after Christmas, or express the doubt he really felt about fighting Mr. Carter at all without knowing something more about him than the part he had considered suitable for publication. He didn't even know whether he could take a joke or not. How would it be now if, as the challenged party, he should state a preference for the broadsword as the weapon to be used—or the quarterstaff? It seemed to him Mr. Carter had reverted to a period when either of them would have been appropriate. The whole business impressed him as being younger than any youth that had ever belonged to him.

It was not until the idea of delay struck him that the prospect suddenly went dark. The thought of death as a possibility was nothing compared to the miserable certainty of being delayed. Even if nobody got hurt—even if the absurd performance ended in the final absurdity of mutual apologies—he still could not get home in time for Christmas. So if he had to kill Mr. Carter it could be for that.

"Journalistic encounter ends in scratch," was the moderate caption under which the episode was recorded several days later in the *Democrat*; the policy on this occasion evidently calling for discretion and for very little else. Hugh, however, had ample time to recall the details from his bed in Mrs. Spottswood's boarding house, for the scratch was his.

There were intervals when without that pain in his leg he might have been led to speculate on the actuality of his recent experiences—to ask whether certain events had really happened—and where—and to whom. Unreality had set in almost from the beginning and had dogged his consciousness throughout the whole affair. The time and the place agreed upon—a misty unfamiliar hour and a wood that he had never seen until he went to it that morning on a horse-car—had seemed to him then as they did now, the sort of rendezvous one makes in dreams. Even the obliging young typesetter who had gone with him as to a bridal, talking all the way, had not succeeded in dispelling the illusion. A battle had been fought at the place they were going to, he had told him among other less arresting things—a real battle—"not just a shooting scrape like this." There was a little church there in the woods where they had carried the wounded and laid them on the benches while the fighting went on outside; he would see it when they got there, the young man said. And Hugh remembered wondering vaguely if they would carry him in and lay him on a bench, or whether it would be Mr. Carter.

Well, it was neither one. There had been the usual preliminaries—usual in books at least—the pacing and the placing, the order given and the answering shot—one shot, Hugh would have said, and would have said he fired it, except for that sharp sensation in his leg. Then he and Mr. Carter were shaking hands and he was being offered Mr. Carter's carriage to go home in instead of the horse-car, because his leg seemed to be bleeding. Better have it attended to, the doctor who was also of the party advised him.

Hugh was careful not to send that copy of the *Democrat* to Mrs. Middleton. Nobody else at home would be likely to hear anything about the duel—he supposed you called it that—until he got there; nor even then if they waited for him to tell it. Some time after New Year the doctor—another doctor—said.

He said it too, in all his letters. Some time after New Year, he told them, things at the office promised to lighten up. Why not just pretend that Christmas came in January this year instead of

December? Certainly there had not been anything where he was to make him think it was coming before that—or even coming at all.

And they wrote back—his mother did—that they would much rather have Christmas in January, for many reasons. For one thing, they were all so busy right now; she hadn't even made the pudding. They would wait until he came to have that and the turkey, and everything. But in the meanwhile, she said (and he could hear a difference in the way she said it), they had something to tell him; something they had been keeping until he came, instead of writing it, but now he might think they ought not to wait that long. Which was a funny thing, when he came to think about it afterward—after he had read the letter over several times—the idea that he would not want to wait even a few weeks longer to have the end of the world thrown at him like that.

But before she told him, his mother wrote—and he could see by the number of pages that the story was a long one—she wanted to assure him that not for one moment had they forgotten the part he had in it all: everything they had thought or said or done, she wrote, had in some way a reference to him and to his happiness, which was as dear to him as it had ever been, or as their own—

He could leave this part until later, Hugh thought; so he left it; he turned the pages and went on.

His mother did not know, she said, how much he had been aware of the change that had taken place this last year in Lawrence's feeling for Anna; she had thought sometimes that no one had noticed it—no one, that is, but herself. She had always been able to understand Lawrence—best of any of her three children. Anna's heart had never been open to her—"and in yours, my darling, I have often been afraid to look."

So there they were, her three children, lined up as for a play. He turned more pages—here it came, the play: the land, the farm—old Adam and his curse. There would be no skipping now; these were the things he had not been told before—the "practical things" that he must not be worried with; the things that bound them to the soil while he went free—and bound them to each other. Debts and mortgages, and the bad years; it seemed to him that in one way or another they must have all been bad; but this last one had somehow managed to outdo the others; it had been the worst. For everybody, his mother said; debtors and creditors alike. Nobody seemed able to explain what caused it, but suddenly there was just no money anywhere. Even the banks—Mr. Houston, after financing her all these years without even a note, had told her he couldn't go on any longer. He didn't want the farm—he had more farms than he knew what to do with—it was the money that had run out. Not Anna's though, she assured him. Thank God, that had not been put into anything.

There were more pages here that Hugh could turn; he knew all about Anna's money; how his mother felt and how Anna felt. It would be the old argument over again—Anna trying to give it to her, and his mother protesting that there was no way to make her touch it—not even borrow it for a month—for a minute. He had heard them go over it; he had listened when they told it to him afterward; he would read on.

He read on. This time they had found a way—a way that one of them at least could take. "—And freely, Hugh," his mother said, "I can look her father in the face with a clear conscience when the time comes and say that Anna chose it herself. It may have been the only way, but she wanted to take it with her whole heart. It may be she had thought of it before—that she was waiting for Lawrence to speak first. There is no telling how long they might have gone on waiting, both of them, if it had not been for this—"

The rest of the letter, Hugh could see, was filled up with himself—his mother's hopes for him, her prayers, her love. He could leave that too.—They were not planning to be married before spring, she said. They were not making any plans until he came. They were not—

He laid the letter down and his face down on it, and tried to think of how he ought to think about what had befallen him. Nobody was dead; nobody was even sick; it didn't seem the kind of thing to pray about.—"O God, don't let her do it!" He was praying now if saying that meant anything; but he didn't expect anybody to hear him. Why shouldn't God let her do it if she wanted to? He told himself he must not think of Anna; he must keep his mind on something else—something with words to it that he could repeat—*Grief brought to numbers could not be so fierce.* Words had always helped him more than anything; he could put himself to sleep with them if something hurt him when he was a child; he had built his castles with them and his forts, and as he grew, they grew. They had made anguish seem a grace and death a glory; maybe that was prayer.

He shut his eyes and pressed his hand over them to make the darkness deeper, but the word written on it was Anna. He saw it as he had learned to write it first with his small fist, as he had seen it written in every language he had learned since then, and in the stars.

His mother's letter had reached him late in the evening, which was in a desperate unreasoning sort of way rather better for him than if it had come at an hour when he would have felt that he might do something about it. Since there was nothing he could do—not at least in the line of going home, with his leg in its present shape—it was just as well for him to wait for morning to realize it.

His helplessness was borne in upon him with the daylight, however, and by the time the doctor had come and found his condition worse than it had promised to be, he plunged immediately into a frenzy of speculation as to how much his failure to go home sooner might have had to do with bringing this disaster upon him—how much it might still be in his power to avert it if he could get there now. He lay and imagined all the ways of going—roads and rivers, swift horses and strong gales; he would have left his leg behind to go.

It was not until several weeks had passed and he had succeeded in adding fever to his other torments—not until the question of a prolonged illness or even permanent disability had brought his mother to his side—that he at length resigned himself to being where he was. He could lie still now and listen; he no longer had to think. His care was now to let his thoughts go by without touching him—afterthoughts of earth; life was something that seemed to have happened to him a long time ago.

It was June before he made up his mind to go home, and they had been married now since February.

He was well, of course; he limped a little, but a man had a right to come back limping from where he had been. Coming back at all was not exactly his idea; he had been convinced a good part of the time that he had a better footing on the ulterior shore.

All the same, he had come back, to take up again where he left off—to pick up the pieces. He felt able to do it, too; he had done a lot of work on himself; morally he did not believe he was limping. Maybe he had been sent back to try it out; in which case he was luckier than most; one chance was the rule.

This time the train was not late, and they were all at the station to meet him—as if he were a hero or something—as if everything had happened to him and not to them—as if being married had not changed anybody in the least. So there he stood with all his armor on before the gates of the city, and the walls were down.

It took a little while for him to feel that he could trust a situation so unexpected, so misleading. He must be on his guard—against what, he did not know; but surely they could not all be back again like this, exactly where they were?

His visit was half over before he saw that the only element of strangeness was the one he brought. As for them, they were, as always, farming. If anything a little more enthusiastically than ever. There were a lot of things they wanted to show him when he got rested up, they told him. And they kept telling him how they hoped now he would stay and not go back to Richmond again. It would be so much better for him. The reference was to his leg; there were no duels around here, was what they meant.

Mrs. Middleton was the only one who ever ventured to bring the duel openly in to the conversation. Why not?—

Since authors sometimes seek the field of Mars,

she quoted from the *English Bards.*

"I am going to be romantic about it whether anybody else is or not," she said. "Would you believe it, Hugh? You are the only man I've ever known to be wounded in a duel—or to fight one, for that matter; though they may not always tell. I doubt whether you would have ever told. But from now on, your recklessness is going to be my blazon and my boast. I am going to have *Ne Crede Byron* for my motto."

This was her way of not asking him questions—about his leg, or about Anna either. It had been a pretty little wedding, she told him.

He saw a good deal of Mrs. Middleton during his visit. There was no element of strangeness there, in spite of the fact that the things they talked of least were the familiar things. He would always be safe with Mrs. Middleton. She would never ask him how he felt about anything that had happened, or even tell him how she felt—or whose fault she thought it had been. And naturally she would never speak again of doing anything for Anna's imagination.

He thought considerably about Anna's imagination; he asked himself just what it was they had both been trying to do with it, and by what right. He thought of her beauty, which had held for him the meaning of all beauty. What had he ever tried to find in that but the thousand images of his own soul? He had not looked for her—for Anna—there nor anywhere; he had loved her because she gave him back himself; not singly but in battalions— he was Cæsar—he was God—but was there any reason why she should love him for that, even though he might be willing to die rather than give it up? Passion that buys with its life the thing it wants may not have been what Anna wanted. Her imagination may have served her well.

The light of day was a strange thing when it fell like this into the abyss where he had sojourned of late; it did not make him see it better; it kept him from seeing it at all. He could have said it no longer existed; certainly not as a place where anything could ever happen to him again—a pit where he might fall another time and struggle and be lost.

PART TWO

THE EMPTY HOUSE

CHAPTER SIX

LAWRENCE AND ANNA had been married almost three years when they bought the Duncan place. It was the first real investment made with Anna's money after what Mrs. Martin called the worst debts had been paid and Nutwood could hold up its head once more. The deed was in Anna's name; it was her place—the only land she had ever owned—and the feeling of satisfaction she got out of it seemed to rise anew with each day's sun. There was something fundamental about it—like finding her center of gravity, Lawrence thought. He knew his mother had always been a good deal like that; maybe it was really women more than men who wanted, so to speak, to own the earth. He had commented on it the afternoon he took Hugh over to see the place.

"It may come from a natural feeling of insecurity—don't you think so? Probably gives them a sense of protection—the way a soft creature builds itself a shell."

"Do for a theory I suppose," Hugh said. "Especially when they stick to their real estate the way Mamma and Anna do. You might carry your idea a little further and say they run the risk of being immobilized along with the other crustaceans. Too much shell."

Lawrence laughed. "Taxable shell at that. The cost of carrying the thing is their last consideration. This place, for instance; it sounds like the biggest kind of a bargain, but by the time you let it lie idle a few years—"

"Whatever became of the Duncans?" Hugh asked him. "I remember the old Colonel—at least I remember seeing him. I don't seem to remember the others much."

"They moved away after he died; to Florida. The only one that was heard from at all in connection with the sale was the oldest son, LeRoy. He put in some sort of protest about it; not offering to do anything of course—anything but make a fuss, that is. He signs himself *Lee*roy. People call him that I suppose, but it's always a bad sign."

"Good pun though."

"I always hate to see a man let his name go like that," Lawrence said.

"Go where?" Hugh said, in memory of Jackson, and added: "Of course I agree with you; being able to spell his own name should always be the boast of the Southern aristocrat. What kind of a row was he threatening to make?"

"Oh, the usual thing: no justice for a patriot's family; ungrateful country—all the rest of it. You might have thought he sounded a little off his head, except there are too many others like him."

"Well, I don't imagine he will get much of a hearing—not all the way from Florida certainly; and anyhow it would have been a pity not to take over the place just on general principles. The house, of course—"

"Of course," Lawrence said; "fixing that up would be out of the question; except for something like an overseer—if we ever got around to having one. It's a pity too; a nice old home. Did you notice the black locusts, there to the north? Anna won't hear to cutting any timber, but, all the same, it is there. She comes over practically every day since we started work on the dam; she would have come with us this afternoon, only I had to take Mazeppa; we are a little short on horses just now on account of the plowing."

Still absorbed, Hugh thought. A dam this time—Mose Alexander, his three sons, two slip-scoops, and four mules, bringing on what looked like one of the minor convulsions of nature in the interest of tomatoes. This time he had been considerably impressed.

He had noticed on all of his recent visits home how much more it took to absorb Anna than it used to do. The family was branching out; every time he came it seemed to him they had gone farther afield. Not that their various interests had ever kept them in what could be called the range of sociability; if they wanted to say anything, they always had to shout; but now if you didn't have a horse you couldn't even relay a remark from one of them to the other. Lawrence had taken more of their own land under cultivation, and Anna, of course, had taken the Duncan place. He didn't know what his mother had taken that she did not have before; but then, she never stayed in the house if she could help it anyhow. Eva was the only one; she was always there. He could tell by the noises Eva made what time of day it was: milk buckets and dishes, and moving the furniture when she swept. If he were not here they would go on just the same—if that was any comfort. Sounds with nobody to listen.

Hugh had not been at home long enough this time to begin thinking of being away again. All the same, he was falling into the rhythm—the beat—that made the days go so fast. He did his writing in the morning; then after lunch he would go to the post office, or out fishing; or maybe go with Lawrence or Anna to admire their respective enterprises, though he had not been able to do that very often so far because there were not enough horses to go round.

It was usually after the first week or two that the days began to follow one another with the fatal smoothness he had learned to recognize, and to dread, because it always brought the end so soon. It seemed strange to him that none of the changes that had taken place in the last three years had changed that feeling in the least. He had noticed that he no longer looked forward to coming back with the eagerness he used to feel, but going away was just as bad as it had ever been; and just as unreasonable. He did not even have the excuse of saying it was something left over from his childhood; he had never been homesick when he was a child, because then he had never been away from home. It had come later, when he was old enough to do something about it; only he could never get hold of it; he couldn't place it; there was something wholesale about it; it was in everything he touched, everything he saw; as if the intention of even the commonest little things had been from the beginning to break the heart. "Once more and this the last—" He was like Othello getting ready to kill Desdemona—he was a fool, but if there is anything that can suffer worse than a fool—Of course in those days it had always ended by just being Anna—as everything else did. And now it must be habit. Most things were habit when you came to think about it; life itself was, if you lived it in one place—watching the shadows fall the same every day from the same trees. It was a terrible risk; a man ought to change his trees.

You are my continuing city—

He had started a poem like that once; something about the gates being no longer shut by night. It was easy to write poetry out of the Bible because it was already written. And now the gates were shut; right in his face; and it hadn't killed him either—the way he would have expected it to do. It had really been good for him: it had opened his eyes to a lot of things; things in Anna, and still more in himself. He could see now that every poem he had ever written to Anna—every thought he had ever had about her, for that matter—had really been about himself. At least he had now reached a point where he could imagine the city continuing without him in it. Somebody else's city. It hurt just as bad as ever to go away, though.

Coming back one afternoon from Pass Christian, where he had gone to mail his morning's work, he had begun to speculate again on the curious relation between monotony and time. It was exactly the opposite of the one commonly supposed to exist; variety, not sameness, was the element that made you conscious of time. Anybody who found it hanging heavy on his hands should just try doing the same thing at the same hour every day and see what happened. Not sleep itself was more oblivious of time than monotony was. This afternoon, for instance: it was about three o'clock now—or would be if he had his watch; three o'clock and all's well. He would find his mother in the bean patch, or some other patch, as usual. Lawrence he would not find at all because as usual he would have ridden off somewhere; and Anna had said as usual that she was going over to see about her dam. Wasn't that her horse, though, there by the gate? Hadn't she gone after all? He quickened his steps; he was near enough now to see that it was indeed Mazeppa; he had Anna's side-saddle on, but no bridle, and was standing outside the gate waiting for somebody to let him in; which was so far from being usual that instead of walking Hugh began to run.

He thought of three things he must do: he must not tell his mother; he must be sure that Anna was not in the house; he must get a bridle and another saddle and go after her. Wherever Lawrence was, he had his horse.

It was not over a mile to the Duncan place, and Hugh did not expect to meet anybody who could tell him anything until he got there. The road ran through the woods almost the whole way; a dirt road, smooth and soundless; not a house in sight on either side. It would be the first gate he came to.

He was surprised to find it open. He knew Anna had ordered it to be kept shut, but he did not stop to shut it now. He could see where the men had been working over on the dam, but there didn't seem to be anybody there; they must have quit work and gone home, leaving the gate open behind them. He kept on to the house.

It was a frame house, built rather like a box, with four front windows upstairs and down, and a front door opening on a square porch. There were trees in the way, and vines, but he was certain he saw somebody on the porch. "Anna!" he called.

It was not Anna; it was a man, a white man, sitting on the top step, holding a revolver loosely between his knees.

"Have you seen a lady over here anywhere this afternoon?" Hugh called to him.

"Come on in," the man called back.

There was a paling fence with a tangle of Cherokee roses on it, and a gate. Hugh threw the bridle over a couple of palings and came on in.

"Leeroy Duncan's my name," the man said without getting up. "I know who you are; you are one of the Martin boys; looking for your wife, or your cousin, or whoever she is."

"Have you seen her? Her horse—"

"I know all about her horse. I sent her horse on home. She was down there at the spring bossing some niggers; I sent them home too."

"Where is Mrs. Martin—where did she go?" Hugh demanded.

"She went where I told her to. Suppose you answer me a few questions. Suppose I've been waiting here for one of you to show up so I could talk over a few things with you—you better keep back— I'm loaded—God damn you—" He jumped to his feet, but Hugh had already passed him. "Anna!" he called into the empty hall.

The doors on either side, leading into the bare rooms, stood open. He turned to the stairs and went up three steps at a time. The two front rooms were shut; their doorknobs had been tied together with Anna's bridle.

"Where are you, Anna?" Hugh said, not loudly this time; he tried to sound conversational; he was untying the straps with hands that shook abominably.

She was in the first room, standing by the front window, her long riding skirt gathered up in one hand; she had been looking down into the yard. "I believe he's going somewhere," she said in a whisper. Hugh had never seen her look so white.

"Well, so are we," he said; "come on."

"No; wait, Hugh. He might not let us. I heard him trying to keep you from coming in. The way he waves that gun
around almost scares me to death. I thought he was going to
shoot Uncle Mose. The boys just ran, and I would have, only he
made me come up here. He sounds like he was crazy, Hugh. He
said—"

"Come on," Hugh urged her. "You can tell me on the way
home."

Anna had turned again to the window. "He's going around
to the back," she said. "Do you think we could get out without
him seeing us?"

"Anna!"

"I know; but I'm afraid of him, Hugh. How do we know he
isn't going to shoot us?"

"How are we going to find out if we don't go down?" he said,
smiling at her. "He hasn't any idea of shooting anybody; I doubt
if his old gun is even loaded. And anyhow we can't stay up here,
Anna. The only thing for us to do is just to walk on down and out
the front door exactly as if he was not there."

"Listen! He's coming in the back door," she said, taking hold
of his arm. "I wish I wasn't such a coward, Hugh."

"I wish so too," he said. "I wonder what you want me to do?
Yelling for help wouldn't do any good. It does look like Uncle
Mose would get somebody and come on back."

Anna looked at him miserably.

"I don't like to leave you," he said. "Do you want me to go
down and get his gun away from him?"

"Oh, don't!" she said. "Please, Hugh—"

"Then come on—that's a good girl! Let me tell you how you
can make yourself do it. Just imagine how you would behave if
you were not afraid at all. Forget about how you really feel; you
can't help that; and act as if you were as brave as—say Joan of
Arc—act it the way you would on the stage. Come on—try it,

Anna; I've done it lots of times. I will go ahead and you keep right behind me."

He saw when he reached the head of the steps that Mr. Leeroy Duncan had indeed come in at the back door and was standing in the hall almost directly below him. Without Anna, the temptation to get the drop on him in a very literal sense by swinging over the banister and landing on top of him might have proved too much for Hugh. Anna had not seen him; he could tell that by the way she was coming on. If he could only get her down before she did see him! He had a sudden inspiration—

"Whoa, you!" he yelled at the top of his lungs. "Just look at that horse trying to pull the fence down! Come on, Anna—" Taking her by the arm he rushed her down the steps and out the front door, noticing as he passed that the hall was entirely empty. The enemy had disappeared.

The yard was empty too, and Mazeppa, who had been doing nothing worse than nibbling at the Cherokee roses, had evidently heard him, for he had stopped doing that.

"I'll lead him over to that stump," Hugh said, "so you can get on behind."

Anna's account of the threats and the bombast indulged in by Mr. Leeroy Duncan did indeed suggest the possibility of his being a lunatic—had anyone cared to put that charitable construction on a style of oratory considerably in use among the sane. It was much more likely that he would turn out to be a rather marked specimen of the bully and coward, or, as Lawrence wearily suggested, just a plain skunk. In any case he could be appropriately dealt with, once the formality of catching him had been accomplished. His disappearance since Hugh had seen him standing in the hall had, however, been remarkably complete. The various search parties, both professional and amateur, that had gone out after him had all returned without him, all equally convinced of the exhaustive nature of their efforts. The country had been combed; the opinion was generally expressed that if Mr. Leeroy Duncan showed up again anywhere it would not be in that neck of the woods.

This was reassuring so far as it went; unfortunately, however, where the Martins were concerned, it was not by disappearing that Mr. Leeroy could cease to be a problem. There was always the off chance of insanity; in which case he could not be counted on to stay away. Not only was it, under the circumstances, out of the question for Anna to continue going over by herself to super-intend the building of her dam; it began to look now as if the dam might not be built—not at any rate in time to carry out the plans they were making for the coming year. Neither Uncle Mose nor his sons were willing to set foot on the place again—"Not after what he done said he was fixin' to do if he ever ketches us back thar," they repeated fervently each time the question came up.

"He's the one that's afraid to be caught there," Lawrence reminded them. "He has quit the country."

"Reckon he's done gone home?" Uncle Mose inquired.

Lawrence would have been glad to reckon that he had, but since he was aware of the fact that Mr. Leeroy had not showed up in Florida either, his general invisibility was all the assurance he had to offer, and that was not enough; the plows and the scrap-ers continued to stand at the same helpless angles on the banks where they had been abandoned, and the deep scars in the earth were being already washed away by heavy rains.

"It must look a good deal like that down in Panama since de Lesseps quit," Hugh said one day when he and Lawrence had gone over to see the extent of the damage caused by the previous night's downpour.

"Pretty bad," Lawrence said. "That's why I didn't want Anna to see it."

"Funny thing for a girl to sink her hopes in a mud-hole like that," Hugh said. "Though I suppose one hole is as good as another when you have to chuck the thing you have been trying to do. Do you suppose that crew would come back to work if we gave them some kind of a guard—got some man over here with a gun?"

"Any white man on the place would do, even without a gun," Lawrence said. "Until they get over their scared fit. I just haven't time to be over here right now."

"I might come a part of the day. I could do my writing up there at the house, I suppose; if you really think that's all they need," Hugh suggested.

"I'm sure it is," Lawrence said. "And then Anna could come on back. As long as she isn't allowed to go and come they are bound to feel there is something to be afraid of."

The return of good weather that befell just then contributed more than anything else could have done to the success of this arrangement. It was not long before Anna had the satisfaction of seeing her earthwork taking shape again and of being herself present at the operation whenever she felt like riding over.

This was usually in the afternoon. Hugh came in the morning. The porch of an empty house had turned out to be a wonderfully propitious place for the kind of writing he was just then engaged in, and by remembering to put an apple and a couple of sandwiches in his briefcase he had found that he did not always have to go home for lunch.

Very little of his time was given these days to the journalism Mrs. Middleton had once deplored; nor had he embarked on the novel, of which she was now beginning to despair. He had been encouraged by a New York publisher—to the extent even of an advance payment—to undertake a collection of literary essays; in which, he told Mrs. Middleton, he was proposing to reset the brightest of those pearls he had been casting before the readers of the *Richmond Democrat*. With this on hand he would feel justified in spending more time at home than he had done since he began working on the paper. He could go on with that wherever he was; the *Democrat* had by this time become one of the habits.

"I can't make up my mind whether they are something to fight against or to give in to," he said. "It's always a temptation to just sit back and let your habits take charge; that gets to be a habit too."

"Doesn't it depend on whether they are good or bad ones?" Mrs. Middleton inquired.

"I'm not so sure of that either. They can change on you—right in midstream so to speak. Sometimes you feel that you ought to turn and start swimming the other way just for the good of your muscles. Even the best kind of a habit gets to be a sort of drifting."

Mrs. Middleton did not say anything. He had something on his mind with which the habit of tossing off copy for the *Democrat* had less to do than other paths of least resistance—she was sure of that. This idea of staying at home more than he used to—was that the sort of drifting he was thinking about?

"Where do you do your writing—I mean when you are over there at the Duncan place?" she asked him presently. "Do you have to sit on the dam, to keep those scared rabbits from running away?"

Hugh laughed. "Not quite; it is more psychological than that. I sit on the porch; I can see the work from there, and see Anna when she rides over. It doesn't really matter where I am, just so I'm there—*à l'œil*, as it were."

"What's in the house—could you go inside if it rained, and have a fire?"

"I haven't wanted one so far," he said; "but naturally there are fireplaces. Nothing in the way of furniture, though. You'll have to come and see it; I know Anna will want to show you her big enterprise."

The porch faced south and so got all the sunshine of the brief winter days. *The sun's low down the sky, Loreena*—the words of the old song were often in Hugh's mind as he watched how small a segment of the great arc it traveled now. The gate was right in the middle of it. Anna would ride in and turn down to the west

79

where the spring was. The dam was solid enough at last for her to ride over it; it was the best way for her to get across. And when she stopped there to watch the work, sitting still in the saddle with the lighted sky behind her and her dark skirt almost touching the ground, she looked as if she were woven in a tapestry. He still saw Anna in all those aspects; that was another one of the things that had not changed; only now he knew it was not in the least because she felt that way—and thank goodness he had stopped expecting her to! That had been the trouble with him all along—the demands he made on Anna's beauty; it had to mean so much. All for his benefit; she had never been interested in the least in meaning all those things.

He always had his own horse ready, so when she finished at the dam and rode on up to the house, all he had to do was to put his papers together and go out to meet her and ride home with her. "Ready?" she would call from the gate.

One afternoon she was early and called to him to wait. "I'm coming in," she said, slipping down from the saddle and gathering up her skirt.

"Sit back where you were," she told him, arranging herself on the top step. "That's a funny table—but just look at the pages you've done!"

He looked at them, and at her. She was sitting just where Mr. Leeroy had stationed himself that afternoon when she was a prisoner upstairs and he was supposedly on guard; he had dangled his pistol a good deal the way she was now dangling her riding whip. Nothing, however, was further from Hugh's mind than to mention it. He was surprised when Anna did.

"I was just thinking as I rode up," she said, "how funny it is the way things turn out. That afternoon when I was shut up in that room up there, I certainly never expected to see you sitting here writing and looking so peaceful, the way you do. That adventure really had a happy ending, didn't it?"

"So far," he said.

"I wish you wouldn't go back to Richmond, Hugh," she said. "We really do need you to stay—if you can write just as well when you are at home as you can up there. We have always counted on your coming back to stay; we talk about it all the time; I reckon we always will—that is, until you do."

He did not say anything. He was putting the pages in his briefcase.

"Do you ever write about people, Hugh?" she asked him after a while.

"Certainly," he said. "I'm writing about somebody now—Shakespeare; you remember him; he was that fellow who—"

"Goose," Anna said. "Mrs. Middleton thinks you ought to write a novel," she went on; "but I don't think you have to do that; if you would just have real people and show them doing something besides writing books themselves. If you would just bring them down to earth more."

"Will you let me write a book about you, if I promise to put the dam in?"

She smiled a little, but she was thinking. "Somebody ought to write a book about Lawrence," she said presently. "Hardly anybody realizes what a beautiful character Lawrence has. I think he must be about the most unselfish person that ever lived. I reckon he gets it from Cousin Louisa in the first place; but a mother is supposed to be self-sacrificing where her children are concerned. Lawrence is unselfish about everybody. People come to him with all sorts of things. It seems to me about all the advice they ever get must be from Lawrence. I hope if we ever have a boy he will be exactly like Lawrence."

"And the girl exactly like Anna? Aren't you afraid of being too original? But I agree with you about the book. What will we have him doing in it? Just what he's doing now? Down to earth, you said."

"Yes, but Lawrence has wonderful ideas, Hugh. He doesn't talk about them much—"

"You mean he thinks? He can't help that, you know—not in real life; he can in a book, though; we don't have to have Lawrence thinking."

"Goose," she said again, smiling at him, then turning back to watch the work that was still going on down at the spring. "You get a good view of it from here, don't you?"

"Fine," he said.

"Has Cousin Louisa told you very much about the money we have made this year?" she asked him. "I know Lawrence has told you some, but he would leave out the most interesting part because he would think it reflected too much credit on him. It has been simply wonderful, Hugh, the way things have turned out for him. And now if we don't lose a lot on what we are planning to do with this place, I believe our troubles will be just about over."

"That does sound like a book," Hugh said. "Like the end of one, though. I always wonder, when we read about people's troubles being over, what they are going to have in place of them. The author just walks off and leaves you to imagine their joys, and in most cases that is hard to do. Let's hear you imagine yours and Lawrence's. Come on—all your troubles are over now, you understand; no more of this early and late business; no more scuffling around to make both ends meet; nobody works except when he feels like it—in an unprofessional sort of way; nobody gets absorbed any more. Somehow I don't believe you are going to like it, unless you have made some plans about what you are going to do instead. Building a new house, for instance; but there you run into work again."

She shook her head. "I know we wouldn't want to do that; or Cousin Louisa either. We could put in improvements, of course. And then of course if we had a family—"

"And that sounds like the beginning of another book, doesn't it?" He picked up the briefcase. "Time to be going; and it looks like another pretty day tomorrow," he said.

CHAPTER SEVEN

WHEN THE WEATHER CHANGED and Hugh had to go inside because his papers blew away, and even to have a fire in one of the open fireplaces, Anna thought it seemed funnier than ever. "I reckon this was their parlor," she said, looking around the big empty room. "We can bring over a couple of chairs and a better table," she suggested. At present she was seated on a box at one side of the hearth.

"Don't make me too comfortable," Hugh said. "I can't see that you need me over here anyhow, now that Mr. Leeroy has turned up in Mexico. Have you told Uncle Mose—or does he know how far away Mexico is?"

She shook her head. "He wouldn't believe it—that he is there, I mean. I'm not sure I believe it myself. Anyhow, I don't want you not to be here when I come over. I wouldn't be afraid, but I would be lonesome; the first thing I do when I turn in at the gate—before I even look over at the dam—is to look up here at the house and think how much nicer it is for you to be here. I keep hoping you can at least stay until we get enough water in the lake for you to see how it is going to look. I believe it's going to be really pretty, Hugh."

He looked at her, smiling.

"Of course it is still muddy now," she went on, "besides being not more than half full, but even so, I noticed when I rode across this afternoon that there were actual little waves on it, with this wind."

"And that from little Anna, who never cared for any waves before!" Hugh said, laughing.

Anna laughed a little too. "It does sound funny, doesn't it?" she said.

"It's all right; it just shows what I've been telling you—that the pleasure is in the doing and not in the done."

She looked thoughtful. "I've been wondering," she said, "just what you do depend on to make you happy—not you especially; I mean everybody. I have always thought that having things not turn out the way you wanted them to, after you have worked over them, made you unhappier than anything; and now you say that no matter how well they turn out they don't make you happy either, because then you lose interest in them—"

"That really doesn't leave you much of a chance, does it? But, after all, just doing things isn't all you have to depend on for happiness," he reminded her. "Take a beautiful day, for instance; think how happy that makes you. As somebody said, all you really need is God and good weather. Not but what that's a good deal, it seems to me."

She was listening in a way that surprised him, so he went on. "Another good way to do is to think about things as if they were happening to someone else, or had already happened, maybe a long time ago—but naturally you can't do that very much while you are still working on them; while you are still absorbed in making them turn out right. I suppose it really takes two people—one to do the thing and the other to look on and get the effect of it—the meaning, if it has one. The *Iliad,* for instance: it took Achilles and Homer both to do that—the way you want me to write about Lawrence."

He smiled, but she was still serious, sitting there on her soapbox.—And speaking of funny things, nothing surely could be funnier than that; for her to be there in the first place, and to be asking him about happiness!

"But you mustn't think about being bored as soon as this," he told her, "now when things are just beginning to come your way. It will be a long time yet before you start losing interest. What you and Lawrence want to do is to go on farming and hire me to look on and write it up—do you some new *Georgics*."

"They were a kind of poem, weren't they?" she asked.

"For a kind of farmer; yes." Hugh said.

The work on the dam was so far completed now that nobody had to worry any longer about its washing away. The rain, for Anna, only meant more water in the lake and seldom meant that she had to stay at home on account of it. For Hugh it meant more fires in the empty parlor, where his pages were being so quickly filled. The idea that he had to be there as a protection had by this time been laid aside; whether Mr. Leeroy was believed to be in Mexico or not, he had crossed another border and was now as little feared as most things are when they have slipped into the past.

"Of course I wouldn't ask Hugh to keep on going over there just for me if it interfered with his writing," Anna said, "but it doesn't, does it, Hugh? There are really not as many interruptions over there as there would be anywhere else, are there?"

These things were true—these negative things—but there was something positive too. Hugh could not deny even to himself that he liked being "over there." It seemed to him that he wrote better in that empty house than he had ever done under any other conditions.

"It is just what I have been telling you all the time," Lawrence now told him again. "There is no reason in the world why you shouldn't write as well here where you belong as you do up there in Richmond. And if you like to have a whole house to yourself while you are doing it, we happen to be in a position right now to accommodate you. And say what you please, Hugh, one of us ought to be over there. If you really have got to go to Richmond, why can't you go now and get back before we start planting? Anna is going to put Uncle Mose to clearing any time now. She's going to want to be over there a lot when the spring work begins."

He would try to come back to finish his book, Hugh told them; he couldn't see much beyond that right now. "But don't let Mamma do any of those things she wants to do to make me 'comfortable'; I can't write when I'm comfortable. And besides, it makes me enjoy the lap of luxury that much more when I fall into it in the evening if I have been sitting all day on something austere like a nail-keg. You all don't realize how soft and padded the life you lead really is."

"I should hope so—compared to the Duncan place."

"Compared to a newspaper office too. The Duncan place is at least clean," Hugh said.

"I am coming to see what you are all doing over there, as soon as you get back from Richmond," Mrs. Middleton told him. "Your mother looks ten years younger, Hugh. This is the kind of thing she has been hoping for all her days. This patriarchal—this matriarchal idea of gathering all her children under her wings to the third and fourth generation. That's a lovely figure of speech, isn't it?—as far as a hen will go along that line! I wish I thought I was going to feel that way about Noel and any one of the girls he has picked out so far—the most abject strangers, most of them. Lots of times I wish I had adopted a daughter-in-law the way your mother did. The longer I live, the more I am inclined to put congeniality ahead of everything—even love—when it comes to making life what it ought to be."

"What ought it to be?" Hugh asked.

"Harmonious, above everything—wouldn't you say? At least you will say it by the time you have seen as many jangling, discordant families as I have. Your family is one of the big exceptions. And just like most of the rare achievements in this world it gives the impression of being perfectly natural; inevitable, you might say. I give your mother a lot of credit, of course, but there is bound to be something behind that—some mixing of the elements she had to deal with in the first place, accidental or—"

"Fatal?" Hugh suggested.

"Hereditary, your mother would say—which may be her name for the same thing. Anyhow it is very unusual. Three young people brought up that way—literally in the woods—and left as free as you all were! Your conduct seemed to have been taken for granted, as far as I can see."

Hugh was listening with interest. "I never noticed us being so good," he said.

"Then notice it now," Mrs. Middleton said. "Of course you don't have to call it being good; I would just as soon you didn't; goodness covers such a lot of things besides the one I'm talking about. I'll find you an epithet—*des qualités,* my grandmother used to say; that is modest enough, at any rate."

"And I can only hope I'm grateful enough," he said. "I would hate terribly to disappoint you, I know that. I'm going to keep an eye on those fugitive and cloistered virtues of mine and not let them give me the slip. Then if my book doesn't disappoint you either—"

Somewhere in this, Hugh was conscious that he was being given a tribute of some sort—a small garland of praise for something Mrs. Middleton imagined he had done. He had probably come off better than she thought he would in the dark turn of events that had overtaken him three years ago—though what she would have expected him to do instead—

They had never gone into that; still it was nice to know she had continued to take a sporting interest in him, since she knew more about how he had felt than anybody else had known. He used to confide in her considerably in those days; it seemed strange to him that he should have told her so much. And yet why not? As long as a man can talk about his feelings they are sure to be pretty well on the surface; they are the kind of feelings that can be a topic of conversation as well as anything else. It is when he has entered the springs of the sea, as Job said, and walked in search of the depth, that he stops talking: there is nothing down there to talk about. Jackson ought to like it down there.

He had wondered a good deal what Anna thought—or if Anna thought—about all those things he used to say to her. What did she think they represented? A state of mind that he could fold up and put away as he would a coat or something that he had outgrown, or that was not suitable any more? She had probably never imagined his feeling for her as anything outside of his control—anything with a life of its own, that would have to be strangled—stabbed—drugged, to keep it quiet. Whatever she thought, it never seemed to bother her. She did not ask how he felt about her now, or ever seem to compare the way he talked to her these days with the way he used to talk. That had apparently dropped back into the past for her. A good deal like Mr. Leeroy—another loud intemperate voice that she did not have to listen to any more.

But suppose she did remember what a fool he used to be, all those years? Suppose she had it in her mind continually, as he could not help having it in his? Surely that would be worse than just forgetting.

He knew he could never explain to Anna in what way his feeling for her had changed, but there were many times when he thought he would like to try. He wanted to tell her that he realized now how selfish he had been—how arrogant—and that he was beginning to learn how impossible it was that beauty could ever belong to him as he had believed it could; even a woman's beauty, that might seem to have been created for him—

> *Oh what are the winds*
> *And what are the waters?*
> *Mine are your eyes!*

He had believed that, but it was not true: even if she had loved him it could not be true; they would always be out of reach—they would always wring his heart.

He could imagine saying these things to Anna, but he did not see what good it would do. She had known all the time that she did not belong to him, or to anybody. And he had lain up there in Richmond and almost died before he found it out. Dying may have been one of the things Mrs. Middleton had thought he might do.

He had been glad for some time now that he had not done it. To have booked that passage, out of simple loyalty to a delusion, might have been a good deal less than was required of him. He had a conviction these days that he was reserved for something more complicated.

Shakespeare and Catullus—he was writing about Catullus now—and other noble madmen long since dead had helped him more perhaps than had the living to regain the footing he had lost. He was not trying to persuade himself that his book was all that was required of him, but he did want to be reserved to finish it. Especially when he got to Richmond and found out how near it came to meeting with Jackson's approval.

"I'm glad to see you sticking to the quieter inflections," Jackson said. "Most interpreters make all the little fishes talk like whales. Did it ever occur to you that if Catullus had lived to be forty he would very likely have burned up the Lesbia poems? I doubt if they seemed like art to him even when he was writing them."

"They probably seemed more like drops of blood," Hugh said.

"I dare say. And some of the 'truculent iambics' still seem more like foaming at the mouth; but that's all right; at least you let him do it for himself. Most commentators think they have to help him; they make him say things that nobody has ever said yet—thank God! I tell you, Hugh, a man has mighty few ideas that can hold up even under one language, and by the time you pile two or three on it, what he meant, or thought he meant, is sure enough sunk; you have to excavate for it."

Hugh smiled. "What you might call the archæological approach?"

"To what you might call bones," Jackson said. *"And, lo, they were very dry.* I don't want to discourage you, though; you are doing a lot better than I could do. *Come from the four winds, O breath, and breathe upon these slain, that they may live."*

Jackson always had plenty of the Old Testament with him, but he only uncorked it, so to speak, on ceremonial occasions. This time Hugh took it to be in the nature of a libation for the book.

He remembered it when he got home and met the impact of the Southern spring. It was the first time in several years now that he had come back in the spring, and to step out of the train, still clutching the briefcase that had contained for him of late what seemed the very reason for his existence, and feel the onrush of this other life that had been all the time preparing, was at first bewildering. Could this be right, unless everything that was not this was somehow wrong? What was this effort he had been making to set his youth apart from the youth of the world? He seemed to be offered some legendary choice in the matter—to be confronted with some miraculous transformation.

He remembered it again when he settled down to work on the porch at the Duncan place, where his mother had assured him he would find everything unchanged; she had only taken the liberty of sending over what she called a more reasonable table and a chair. She saw nothing unreasonable in the white sheets of Cherokee roses that had been hung out on the fence nor the clouds of honeysuckle now pink against the sky. Come from the four winds, O breath—

The water in the lake was clear now, or almost clear, and the banks were almost green. It was every bit as ornamental as Anna had thought it might be, but her interest now lay farther afield, where the planting was in progress. He looked to the east to see her now.

"It makes the biggest difference, Hugh, having you back," she said. "It used to give me the strangest feeling to come over here and not find you. I would begin to remember about it before I got to the gate even—that you wouldn't be here—and yet somehow I always expected to see you. I do hope you have got everything fixed so you won't have to go back to Richmond. How is your book getting along? Are you still writing about Shakespeare?"

Anna talked more than she used to—more to him, at least; she even listened more. Not about Shakespeare, though; that was just politeness. One day when it rained and she had to take refuge on his porch, she revealed the fact that she also remembered more.

"One day while you were gone," she told him, "when I rode over sort of late, such a funny thing happened; at least, I thought it happened. I had been thinking about you as I came along— about something you had said—and after I finished telling Uncle Mose what I wanted him to do next, down at the dam, I rode on up here. And do you know, Hugh, I could have sworn I saw you, here on the porch, sitting just the way you are now? It seemed so natural it didn't even scare me; not at first. Of course when I realized it wasn't anybody, I began to feel sort of queer; I began to wonder if something might have happened to you, like that time—" Anna had never mentioned the duel to him. She did not mention it now.

"That is what the Germans call a *Doppelgänger,*" he told her. "It isn't supposed to be lucky—for the person who has it, I mean; it is all right for the one who sees it. This time it doesn't seem to have hurt either one of us, does it? I got back from Richmond safe and sound and you were not too much frightened to turn around and gallop home, were you?"

"I didn't gallop," Anna said. "I wanted to think."

She seemed to be thinking now. "Does writing make you happy?" she asked him after a while.

"Do you mean while I'm at it?"

She nodded. "Yes—all these hours you sit here. I can always tell about Lawrence—whether he is worried about anything or not."

"And you can't tell about me? Do I look worried when I am writing?"

"You always stop before I can tell. When I used to hear you and Lawrence talk about what you were going to do—I mean a long time ago," Anna said, "before you started writing—I didn't realize what a different sort of thing it was. I thought it was more like sewing—something you took up and put down again. It's really more like just not being here, isn't it—like being somewhere else?"

"You mean it is not very sociable?" he said, smiling at her. "Mamma thinks that too; and so does Mrs. Middleton; she says she is coming over to see about it. But being happy and being sociable are not the same thing. You asked me whether I am happy or not, and I can answer that—in a way. I can say that at least I am a great deal happier than I thought I was going to be, awhile back."

"And when you finish this book you can begin another one, can't you? You can always do that?"

"That's the idea exactly," he said, smiling. "Start right over again, just like farming."

CHAPTER EIGHT

"AND WHERE, may I ask, is Anna?" Mrs. Middleton had finished with the view from the porch, where she was occupying the chair, and now brought her glance back to Hugh, who was sitting on the steps.

He looked at the sun. "It's about time for her to be coming," he said. "We can't see her from here; the field is on the other side of that thicket."

"Her pond—excuse me, lake—is rather pretty, isn't it? Does she really expect to water things with it?"

"She's got her pipes all laid. The thing she's afraid of now is the weather going back on her."

"How do you mean?"

Hugh laughed. "Anna's afraid there won't be any drouth this summer; she's never known a summer when there wasn't, but she thinks it could happen, and then where would she be? All that water and nothing to use it for."

"That would be funny, wouldn't it? It's been about the loveliest spring I ever remember—if that's any comfort to her," Mrs. Middleton said.

She looked over at the strip of tangled woodland, the bushes, and the vine-draped trees that cut off the view of Anna's activities. One could hardly imagine anything as purposeful as agriculture going on so near at hand, soundless and invisible like that. It was the stillest hour of the afternoon. The shadows lay full-length across the grass, and in one of them Mrs. Middleton's carriage waited—the very image of repose, with the horses standing motionless and Uncle Isaiah on the front seat sound asleep. Peace, she thought—or what should be peace.

A breeze moving through the open door behind her stirred the papers on the table, where Hugh had been at work. He got up and collected them, putting the copy of Catullus on top of them, then took up again his easy attitude on the steps.

"I suppose you never think about its being too still, do you?" she asked him. "Claud Devore—the painter, you know—used to say he couldn't paint when he came to see me because it was too quiet, and my house is noisy compared with this. He used to get the cook's children to come around and play under the window. But then of course he was not talking to old lovers' ghosts the way you are; Catullus wouldn't want Mandy's children."

"I expect a painter likes to be reminded of the Latin Quarter," Hugh suggested, smiling up at her. "I was reading somewhere about a sculptor who used to work with the faucet dripping in the bathroom to remind him of his Roman fountain—until his landlord got the water bill."

"Well, of course art is a mystery," Mrs. Middleton said, "but it doesn't seem to be the getting away from life that it is supposed to be. It has to keep where it can be reminded of what is going on—or else it turns into a sort of sleepwalking. Which a good deal of it is, according to my idea."

"I thought right now it was supposed to be too wide awake," Hugh said. "But of course I see what you mean. It's a sort of border-line business, any way you look at it—a calculated distance between the artist and what he thinks of as nature."

"Maybe," Mrs. Middleton said; "but I believe keeping the distance isn't as important as keeping something always between; not footlights exactly—"

"Masks? Costumes? Surely not anything artificial for art! You don't want your artist to be just a disinterested spectator, do you?"

"No; just the opposite; interested; the only one who can be really interested because he is the only one who really sees the thing. I'm no artist, but I know that is the only way to enjoy practically anything—the best way to keep it from getting you down. I remember the first time I ever went to the theater—and I wasn't so young at that, but I have never suffered such anguish in my life as I did over that silly play. I didn't half see it; I just sat there and believed it—and boohooed my head off."

"That's dreadful," Hugh said. "Mistaking art for reality. I know your grandmother was ashamed of you."

"All the same, it taught me a lesson," Mrs. Middleton said. "I learned right then and there to reverse the process. Whenever things got too bad for me after that, I just pretended I was seeing them on the stage. How did I know it was not acting, I used to say to myself. Even now I can imagine coming back some time and seeing everything over again. Did you ever think of that, Hugh—of how much more discriminating we would be the second or third round?"

"I wonder if we would," he said; after which they were silent for a while, both of them looking at the thicket.

"What is Anna going to plant over there besides tomatoes," Mrs. Middleton presently inquired, "or do you know? How much do they let you in on all of this—" she waved her hand comprehensively at the landscape.

"Not very much, I'm afraid. My attitude is a good deal the one you advocate—seeing and not believing."

"Still, you do have your agricultural side, don't you?"

"In abeyance. I'm being kept in reserve for some future contingency. Just what, I don't know."

"Well, see to it that they don't get you into it unless they have to. Keep that thicket between you and—whatever it is—as long as you can. Yonder comes Anna now."

She was off of her horse by the time Hugh got to the gate. Mrs. Middleton watched them coming up the walk together. "I didn't know Hugh had company," Anna called to her. "I couldn't see the carriage from where I was; I hope you haven't been here long. Hugh ought to have whistled for me."

"You wouldn't have heard me. It isn't so still over there in the field," he told Mrs. Middleton. "When Anna isn't bossing her hands they are bossing each other."

"Or singing," Anna said. "I'm so glad you have come to see everything. Hugh told me you had been promising to come."

There was no chair for Anna; she sat on the steps too, looking up at Mrs. Middleton. The long black calico skirt she had put on over her blue dress hung below her very much as it did from the saddle. She had taken off her hat and put it over her knee. It was a leghorn hat—not her best, but it had been her best and still wore around its crown a faded wreath of cornflowers and roses. Looking at this pale garland and then at Anna, Mrs. Middleton had the queer impression that she had drunk its freshness up—drained its colors like a glass. *Dieu, que tu es belle!* She had heard her grandmother say that more than once to some girl arrayed for a party. She would no doubt have said it to Anna, arrayed or not, if she had seen her now. Her grandmother had no mercy; she would not have given a thought to Hugh, sitting there at the other end of the step; or if she had, it would only have made her worse. She would not have felt that she ought to talk about something else—look at something else—anything rather than call attention to Anna.

"How long have you had the gypsies camping there by the gate?" she said, that being the first thing she could think of, and looking at the gate.

"Just today," Anna said. "Maybe just this afternoon. Were they there this morning when you came, Hugh?"

"There wasn't anything there. What kind of gypsies?"

"The usual kind," Mrs. Middleton said. "They told me they came from Pascagoula. I asked them where they were going, but they wouldn't commit themselves that far. Anyhow, I had my fortune told. I never miss a chance of doing that."

"Who told it? I didn't notice anybody that looked like that," Anna said.

"They always have somebody like that. This time she was rather good. She told me about Noel."

"What did she tell you about him?" Anna asked.

"Oh, the usual thing—that I had a son and—I don't remember whether she said he was not married—"

Hugh laughed. "I wonder how much you paid her for telling you you had a son. Didn't you know it?"

"Yes, but she didn't; that's why I say she was good. They haven't been in the neighborhood long enough to hear anything about any of us. You ought to go right away, Anna, if you want her to tell yours. Hugh doesn't, of course. I think your lake is lovely," she added, getting up. "Ask her if we are going to have a drouth right away, so you can use it. Go wake up Isaiah, Hugh; tell him I'm ready."

"Sit down for a minute while I get my horse," Hugh said. "We'll escort you part of the way."

The road, when they got outside of the gate, was too narrow for outriders. "So Isaiah and I will drive along," Mrs. Middleton said. "Go on over there and get Anna's fortune told"—she nodded toward the gypsy camp. "They may be gone in the morning. That one cooking supper is the fortune-teller." She waved her hand and departed.

There were two tents in the edge of the wood, with a wagon, a cart, and the requisite assortment of livestock and human beings. Garments of many colors hanging out to dry betokened the perpetual washday of a caravan, and the iron pot swung over a fire promised its evening meal. It was picturesque—Hugh admitted that—but he did not think, as Anna did, that it looked mysterious.

"They are not gypsies, to begin with," he said. "They are just ordinary stragglers. You don't really want to say anything to them, do you, Anna?"

"But look at the one over by the fire—the one Mrs. Middleton said. Don't you think she looks like a gypsy, or at least an Indian? Let's just ride in there a minute—let's ask that man there by the wagon."

"Ask him what?" Hugh protested; but the man, noticing their hesitation, came forward with a question of his own. He wanted to know if there was any objection to his camping in the gentleman's woods for that night.

"Certainly not," Hugh told him. "In the first place it is not my wood."

It was not too near the gentleman's gate? He addressed Hugh, but he looked at Anna. "And the lady would have her fortune told, no? My mother ees first-class to tell fortunes." His mother, or at any rate the woman Mrs. Middleton had indicated, having now joined them, he finished with a gesture and withdrew.

Hugh turned to give Anna a deterring glance, but realized he might just as well bestow it on the horse from which she was already descending. He dismounted too and stood beside her, feeling as foolish as possible and fishing in his pocket for the traditional silver piece with which the foolishness was supposed to begin. The woman's palm, however, was not extended; she stood quite still, looking from one of them to the other with a pair of very remarkable eyes. Indian—Cajun—she could have been any one of a number of things, and probably was several of them, he reflected.

"*M'sieu et Madame* are not at home in that house from which they come?" she said presently, in a tone so conversational, so entirely at variance with her exotic appearance, that the usualness itself was startling. Anna looked at Hugh, waiting for him to speak, then back at the woman and said: "No."

"The *maison* of *M'sieu et Madame*—I will describe to you your house," the woman said. "It is grander than the one there." She waved her hand toward the gate. "It has many rooms and many windows; it has a high roof and there are two towers; and about it stand many trees. There *M'sieu et Madame* have lived since childhood, and will live there *toujours*. Their children—I will describe to you your children. The boy—"

Anna looked at Hugh again. "Hold on a minute," he began; but the woman's eyes were far away, and so apparently were her ears; she went on as if he had not spoken.

"The little boy is like M'sieu, with a dark face and many thoughts—an artist perhaps? The little girls—" she held her hand down in three gradations.

"But we are not married," Anna now broke in—"not to each other."

This time the oracle was more attentive; she looked vaguely troubled. It was a little while before she spoke again. "But today and tomorrow—how can I know? They are all one, madame—" She stopped.

They waited, but she did not go on; until presently, as if the conversation had now reached its end, she inquired casually: *"M'sieu et Madame* are pleased with the fortune?"

"How much ought I to give her?" Hugh asked. "Or here— you do it." He handed the loose silver he had brought up from his pocket to Anna, taking the bridle from her arm, and stood back between the two horses while she said her thank-you and good-by.

"Better hop on," he told her then; "we are going to be late for supper."

"Didn't it make you feel funny, Hugh?" she began as soon as they got back to the road. "Wasn't it the strangest thing for her to know all that—about where we live—and the way she described the house—"

"What was strange about the way she described it?" he said. "It is that kind of a house."

"But when she had never even seen it, Hugh—don't you remember Mrs. Middleton said they had just come, from the other direction—not that way? She couldn't have seen it."

"What makes you think—or Mrs. Middleton think—this is the first time she has ever been around here? You don't know how many times she may have tramped over this road."

"Oh—I hadn't thought of that," Anna said. She looked thoughtful. "Then maybe she had seen us before, too. But all the same—" She stopped.

"It's an old game, Anna."

She didn't say anything. For a while they rode in silence; then Anna asked him: "Do you suppose Mrs. Middleton believes it, Hugh—that it is really second sight or something?"

"I think she likes to think she does."

"And I suppose they always tell you something they think you want to hear, don't they?"

"They generally try. They probably slip up occasionally."

They were almost home now. When Anna spoke again it was to say something about the weather and her plans for tomorrow if they had another nice day. "I never saw so many, all in a row this way. It has been the loveliest spring!"

The subject was changed; he knew that, but he did not realize it had been abandoned. He was surprised when she did not mention the gypsies again—not in his hearing—at any time during the evening. And the next morning when he rode back rather earlier than usual, he saw as he passed that they were breaking camp.

The beautiful days continued. Anna had never seen so many. And Catullus—

For us, when the one time our little light has set—

Those Roman springs were probably not unlike this, Hugh thought. Climate—weather—was a tremendous bond between men and countries; and between the ages, too. Having the seasons fall the same was like hearing tunes that were familiar. If understanding how Catullus felt was a help in trying to write about him—

"Do you remember, Hugh, what that gypsy said about today and tomorrow being all the same thing?" Anna had asked him to ride over to the dam with her on their way home, and then she wanted to get off and sit on it awhile, the better to admire the clearness of the water. One could see almost to the bottom now; it was really very clear. What had reminded her of today and tomorrow? He thought a moment before he answered.

"Wasn't that what she said—just that they were the same? I don't remember her saying anything else about it," he said.

"Yes, but just what were the words?"

" 'Today and tomorrow are all one,' was what she said. I don't know what she meant, unless it was some excuse she might have been making about—well, about pretty much everything she had been telling you. I thought you had sort of put her off your mind by this time."

Anna did not say anything. She was looking down at the water, which, as so often happened with the things she looked at, gave her back the color of her eyes.

"Don't you remember," he went on, "how the old oracles used always to give the people who consulted them such muggy answers—so nobody could ever pin them down?"

She had stopped looking at the lake now and taken him into her eyes—*Occidit brevis lux.*

"And anyhow," he said, getting up, "it is time we were going. We can talk about it on the way home."

"No, Hugh; it isn't all that late; look at the sun! And besides, this is something I want to ask you."

He sat down.

"I never used to think very much about the past and the future," Anna said, "or the present either, for that matter. I never even noticed where one of them left off and the other began."

"Hardly anybody does, do they?" he said encouragingly.

"I thought maybe you did; you have so much more time than other people seem to have—for things like that, I mean. I never thought how small the present is, compared with the future, or the past either. When you look forward it always seems as if there were ever so many things you could do, instead of there being just one; and it's the same when you look back—you see ever so many roads you might have taken instead of the one you did take. And yet all the while I suppose there never is but one."

"There never is but one at a time, certainly; but you can keep on changing it; in fact, you have to keep on changing it even if you don't want to—so you get plenty of variety in the end. Imagine yourself in the middle of something like—you know an hourglass?—with more sand than you can count on either side of you, but you have to take it one grain at a time. You can choose your grain—at least you think you can—but whether you pick a bad one or a good one you are not going to be able to hold on to it. At least that is one way of looking at the situation. There are plenty of others."

To see Anna taking an interest in the things that are unseen was a new experience. He wondered what could have started her off like that. The gypsy must have had something to do with it, but even so—Anna, the way she used to be, might have met the occult in a more impressive form than that without being half as much impressed. She would have laughed it off, or at any rate have talked it off; it would never have occurred to her to keep it to herself and brood over it this way.

"Everybody feels sometimes that he would like to go back and start over from somewhere," he told her; "he can generally pick the very spot he would like to get back to. It's one of the best ways in the world to make yourself miserable. But I can't imagine why you want to experiment with it. Surely you are not regretting anything you have had a hand in so far—the way it has all turned out? All this, for instance—I thought you brought me over here to show me how nice it all was."

"I know; it has all been wonderful, hasn't it? And just last fall do you remember how worried I used to be for fear the dam might break? I really have been awfully lucky, Hugh; we all have. I expect we had better be going."

Lawrence said the same thing: that they had all been remarkably lucky. "Things are a whole lot better for everybody just now," he told Hugh. "And the Lord knows the country is entitled to a little burst of prosperity—especially this part of it. The danger now is in being too sanguine—having too much at stake when things start down again, as of course they are sure to do. On the other hand, now is the time to improve our position as much as we can—with safety. And certainly now is the time for you to be here. In fact, Hugh, if you could see your way to taking over this Duncan place—"

Lawrence had ridden over to see about the planting and was now sitting on the porch proposing the very thing Hugh had been afraid he was going to propose. He had begun, of course, by asking him about his book, which he wouldn't do anything to keep him from finishing, he said. They always had to get the book out of the way before Lawrence ever settled down to business.

"But you know," he proceeded, "to make an undertaking like this remunerative is a bigger job than Anna imagines. Anna has more judgment than almost any man I know, but all the same this is a man's job, and, as I say, if you could take it over—"

Hugh shook his head. "From what I've seen of Anna since I took this porch over, I believe she would rather run her own place on a small scale and lose money on it than to turn it over to anybody else—even somebody a whole lot better equipped than I am to run it on a big scale and make it pay. What would she do with the money that she would enjoy doing half as much? Don't you remember, we talked it over before—"

"But this way, Hugh, Anna wouldn't have to feel that the place had been taken out of her hands—as it would be if I turned it over to a manager. This way she could come over and look after it just as much as she does now. That's the thing that has made it possible all along—the fact of your being here. She knows that; we all do—you know it too. And it's the only thing I can think of that will make it possible for her to go on with it. Don't make up your mind about it now; wait until your book is out of the way. I just want you to be thinking it over."

Lawrence got up, holding his hat and his riding whip, and stood looking out over the landscape in that special way a man has of looking at what he understands; not appraisal altogether, and yet not just idle admiration. What was it exactly? Hugh wondered. "All right," he said; "I'll be thinking it over."

Lawrence did not go; he stood awhile longer; there was something else he wanted to say.

"That question of what we would do with the money," he began. "It seems to me what I would like better than anything would be to swap off some of it for a little more time. Time to read something besides the *Country Gentleman* once in a while. A lot of things I always planned to do seem to be getting pushed to the wall these days."

He looked down at the table where Catullus was lying on his face among the scribbled pages, and Hugh, sitting on one corner of it, looked at him. Land was not the only thing Lawrence knew the value of. He was the aristocrat of the family; there was no getting around that. There was a sort of integration about his way of choosing the best—in everything. The life he had chosen in the first place, and the looks that went with it—or at any rate the clothes. Lawrence was what Mrs. Middleton would call harmonious. And if he did get more time for reading, that would be as becoming to him as the rest; the Thomas Jefferson sort of thing, the agrarian dream; leisure to go beyond his own fields and reap where he had not sown. Time really was the hardest thing for the country gentleman to come by these days; but Lawrence would probably manage that too. As Anna said, in the future there were ever so many things you could do. It was only in the present that they got pushed to the wall.

He started to write again after Lawrence had gone, but instead he found himself wondering just what it was that made such a deadly difference between writing and doing any of the other things people did; the things they spoke of in a composite sort of way as working, or just as living—the things that Lawrence did, and Anna, and pretty much everybody around here. Writing after all might not be exactly living; it might be more in the line of a suspension of that responsibility. Like being somewhere else, Anna said. Maybe it was; maybe it was being in a place where today and tomorrow really were the same; where the present was no longer small.

And he was being invited to come back where the hours would have significance again; no more planetary pauses. Life as they understood it was being once more assigned to him. Because they loved him, because they did not want to let him go, they had worked out this way of keeping him. It was like looking back and seeing the other roads he could have taken—and all the time there never was but one.

CHAPTER NINE

WHEN MRS. MIDDLETON heard about the plan—not from Hugh but from his mother—and showed so plainly what she thought of it, Louisa seemed genuinely surprised. It had not occurred to her that they were "asking a good deal of Hugh"; she had not even called the plan a plan; she had spoken of it as their hope. There was no use in explaining to Louisa that the hope was what you had before you made the plan—though of course you could go on hoping for the plan to work out. Which was what Louisa was doing; though she said they would never ask anything of Hugh that was not for his happiness—and couldn't Mrs. Middleton see how much happier he was here at home than he had been in Richmond? For Louisa, Richmond was associated not only with the newspaper and with duels but also with Mrs. Spottswood's boarding house. She had remarked more than once that belonging to a good family didn't always make a woman a good housekeeper, even in Virginia.

It seemed to Mrs. Middleton, however, that in spite of these disadvantages Richmond was a better place for Hugh at present than home, whether he was happier there or not. She would have liked to mention the fact that even in Mississippi belonging to a good family did not always make a young man an angel.

And certainly Louisa did not have to remind her that Hugh's happiness, and Lawrence's too, had always been her main object in living; there never was a moment when she would not have given the last drop of her blood for either one of them. But, all the same, that had not kept her from giving both of them, bound hand and foot, over to a girl like Anna to do what she pleased with. She had begun it when they were too little to help themselves, and, as far as Mrs. Middleton could see, she was still doing it.

Of course when she said a girl like Anna, she was naturally thinking of the way Anna looked more than of anything she really was; but in the case of a boy like Hugh that was enough. He didn't have to know what the moon really was either, to go on wondering at it. And how could being married make such a difference in the situation? Making Anna inaccessible. For a poet that was the last thing you wanted to do—that "for ever wilt thou love, and she be fair" business!

Altogether it was the kind of situation you would expect to come across back in the days when people had to stay in one place and work things out for themselves—against the gods, so to speak. All in the family too, with no lines drawn to keep one thing from running into another.

It really looked sometimes as if that practical point of view which worked so well for Louisa in almost everything else had a way of forsaking her in the most surprising manner when it came to a question of people's behavior—especially young people. Maybe associating too much with nature gave you an exaggerated estimate of human nature. Marble men and maidens. "Don't ever forget that even a gentleman is a man"—she remembered her grandmother telling her that, though she had never gone on to say what a man was.

It occurred to Mrs. Middleton that it might not be such a bad idea after all to set a girl to memorizing all those pages of French poetry she had been made to learn when she was too young to understand it in the least—so that it would come back to her when she did. Racine, for instance:

C'est Vénus toute entière
à sa proie attachée.

And yet, for some reason, when you saw anybody taking virtue as a matter of course the way Louisa did, you felt ashamed not
to do it too. There must be something noble about believing—
really believing—almost anything: saints in flesh and blood,
angels in plumes and armor—Mrs. Middleton began to think it
might be easier after all to talk to Anna. She hadn't seen Anna
since she had her fortune told.

"I suppose the gypsies have gone?" she said to Louisa.

"What gypsies?"

It was when Louisa said that to her that she knew it was time
to talk to somebody. Too much reticence was always a bad sign
in a family.

"I have been meaning to come and tell you," Anna said. "It
was the strangest thing! I had no idea it would make me feel the
way it did. Do you know, she told me right off that she knew
I didn't live up there at the Duncan place, and then she began
to describe Nutwood—the house and the trees and everything,
exactly as if she were drawing a picture of it; looking right at me
all the time. It gave me the feeling she must be seeing it in my
eyes."

"And what did Hugh say?"

"He said she had seen it already—that it couldn't be the first
time she had been here. He doesn't believe anything—he doesn't
believe that you do either. That is what I wanted to find out—
whether you really do think it is second sight or something—"

"Certainly I do. Hugh just has to be strong-minded. Men
always have to pretend not to believe things. Did you ask her
anything else—about your lake, for instance?"

Anna shook her head. "We didn't get around to that. We only
had a minute; Hugh said we would be late for supper."

"Well, next time I'll go with you myself; they may be back. How do you feel about turning your place over to Hugh, Anna? I thought you wanted to run it yourself."

"I do—I am; I mean we are going to do it together." Anna looked at her with unclouded eyes.

There was a short silence, and then Mrs. Middleton said: "Anna, I am going to speak to you quite frankly; it's about Hugh. You know I have always been more interested in Hugh than in any of the rest of you; in some ways even more than in Noel. I have always thought he had a brilliant future; I still think so."

She waited and Anna waited too.

"I wonder if you know," Mrs. Middleton went on, "how much Hugh used to talk to me, all that time he was so in love with you—when he thought he might marry you? I always thought I understood better than you did how much it meant to him. I was afraid of what it might do to him to have to give it up."

Anna was looking at her attentively. "Cousin Louisa thought that too. She really worried about it; but then he was so sick after that, and that worried her so much more—I suppose he just got over everything together," Anna said.

"But he still limps a little sometimes; you have noticed that, haven't you? Maybe there is something that always remembers. Maybe we never get over things completely, if they have hurt us very much. Especially when we are young—or if we happen to be like Hugh. What I want to ask you now is whether you are not afraid that being with you a great deal—seeing you constantly, the way you are planning to let him do—may make it harder for him to forget—that he might begin to feel about you as he did before."

"But he couldn't now, could he?" Anna asked her. "I mean he never would—"

The idea was so evidently new to her that for a moment Mrs. Middleton regretted having presented it; but only for a moment. She decided then that since she had done so and since her eyes were already on Anna's face, she would just keep them there until something happened. Anna was not a child; she was a married woman; she had no business to sit there as remote as all that.

Very little did happen. A silence ensued, and in the end Mrs. Middleton had to make what she could of the slow wave of color that crept up from Anna's little white collar to the edge of her smooth hair. This was, however, more in Anna's case than it would have been in a girl more given to blushing.

"And then of course the great consideration of his career," Mrs. Middleton proceeded. "I may be taking a one-sided view—Hugh's side. The rest of you may have all sorts of reasons for keeping him here that I know nothing about; but I can't see how any of them could be so important that it ought to be allowed to interfere with his writing; especially just at this juncture."

Anna, still dyed with her blush, looked up; she knew the formula for this.

"But he is going to finish his book first," she said. "Lawrence wouldn't let him not do that; none of us would."

Mrs. Middleton looked at her meditatively for a moment and then asked a question—not because she thought Anna would know the answer to it, but because she wanted to remind her that for Hugh at least it had an answer:

"Could you tell me, Anna, just what reason there is why Hugh should stay here and be a farmer, after all the time he has given to preparing himself for another sort of life altogether? I am thinking of practical considerations, not sentimental ones; I know of course how your mother feels about it. To be perfectly frank with you, Anna, I am wondering just what argument Lawrence has used. Does he really need some one to take over, out there at the Duncan place?"

This time Anna hesitated.

"As I say, I know how your mother feels," Mrs. Middleton repeated. "It is only natural for her to want to keep all of you with her; in her eyes, Hugh belongs here as much as he ever did."

"But he feels that way too," Anna broke in. "He has always hated to go away worse than anything. Has he never told you? It was only the question of money; and now that things are so much better, Lawrence thinks—we all think—he ought to stay. He really does belong there; it isn't just on account of the Duncan place. Nutwood is his home just as much as it is ours. Even the gypsy said that, when she was describing it—"

Mrs. Middleton was watching her with interest. "You didn't tell me that," she said quietly when Anna suddenly stopped. "What else did she say?"

"Just that—just that she always saw him there," Anna told her; and this time her lovely face was colored with what Mrs. Middleton took to be a lie.

So there they were: Anna, no more given to lying than to blushing, was doing both. What had happened to her? Such commotions seemed as out of place in Anna as if she had taken to, say, frizzing her hair. They did not go in the least with her usual behavior—with that sort of half-conscious, enchanted way of doing things that seemed always to leave her out of them no matter how much she got other people in. There were a lot of women like that, Mrs. Middleton thought—just put in to make it harder; only you didn't notice them so much unless they happened to be beautiful. Then Fate got into it. It was when they had the look of the Immortals, as Homer said, that people began to be afraid of them and to feel that there was something unpropitious in having them around; sensible people, that is; not poets. Women like that were just made for poets; certainly they were the kind they always made for themselves.

And of course in this case Hugh was the one who ought to be getting out of the way; he knew that as well as anybody did. If only they didn't make it so hard for him! Even Lawrence.

It was when she got to Lawrence that Mrs. Middleton became conscious of a disposition to withdraw a little. Proceeding along that line had a tendency to make her pause and take stock of certain possibilities that she felt unfit to deal with by any light she knew—even those far-reaching beams that followed in the wake of her French grandmother. She could not imagine herself talking to Lawrence about any phase of this business, no matter what turn it took; no matter how many things she saw that she was sure he did not see; even if she saw him laying the ax right at the root of his family tree. All she could do when it came to Lawrence was just to shut her eyes and hope for the best—and try not to remember some of the things that happened in families.

In the middle of the thicket that cut off the view of the tomato field there was a marble obelisk; not a tall one and considerably hidden under the encroaching vines, but important enough, presumably, to keep away any depredations other than nature's from the Duncan family's burying ground.

Almost any thicket near anybody's house in that luxuriant climate was more than apt to indicate a place that had at one time been set apart either as a flower garden or a burial plot; since all ground that did not go under the plow went almost immediately under some swift form of vegetation, and the most favored places were likely to be more choked than others by the very shrubs and flowers that had been put there to sweeten and adorn them. Still, nobody had thought of the thicket in that connection. The jungle that was once the garden showed glimpses of white blossoms among the heavy foliage, and Anna had gone a little way along the dark walk leading into it, thinking all the while of snakes; but the thicket had not been investigated until one day the dogs went in after a rabbit—Uncle Mose's dogs, who spent their endless leisure lying in the furrows where the earth was cool and dreaming no doubt of rabbits, until now and then a real one, or perhaps only the smell of one, would chance to come their way.

Anna liked this to happen when she was present; it was the most exciting thing imaginable, though bad for the tomatoes. The dogs just took straight off across the field, yelping their heads off, and the boys, and even Uncle Mose, didn't notice very much where they were putting their feet when they started after the dogs. Anna had never seen them get the rabbit, but none of them, not even the dogs, ever looked the least bit discouraged in consequence.

They did not get it on this occasion either, but she noticed that they came back a little subdued; and then Uncle Mose told her about the graveyard. "So we called 'em off an' come on out befo' we cotch him," he said.

It seemed very interesting. Anna told him that later on when they had more time she thought they ought to get it cleared and trimmed up—but couldn't he and the boys cut her enough of a path to go in there now and see the monument? Uncle Mose said they sho' could.

"Don't you know it must have been lovely?" she said to Hugh, who went with her. "Not the monument—I mean the place, the way they had it planted. It's even pretty now; did you ever see so much yellow jasmine!"

Hugh was reading the inscriptions on the obelisk. "Listen," he said. Colonel Duncan's virtues had been recorded in what he called the Roman manner. It sounded to Anna as if Mr. Leeroy might have written it.

The eulogy on the opposite side in memory of Mrs. Duncan was more poetic and had evidently been composed by the Colonel himself. It was long, and the letters were small—in the copybook manner—and now black with time. She must have died a long while ago; maybe while she was still young and beautiful, Anna thought. The things he said about his "beloved wife" impressed her deeply.

"I hope Lawrence will think up something as beautiful as that for me," she said—"*Thou thine earthly task hast done.*"

"Shakespeare thought up that part of it," Hugh told her.

"Oh—well then, no wonder," she said.

"But five children, Anna—" Hugh was reading on another side—"five besides the ones who lived to grow up; she couldn't have been very young."

There were no inscripitons for the children other than their names and dates; no eloquence for five little graves among the vines; he was glad of that. "Don't you think we have seen enough for this time?" he asked.

Anna said yes, but she did not move. "Another thing I never used to think about," she began presently, "is how good you have to be—I mean how people have to stand so much, and still go on with their lives even when they must be so sad."

"But they have a lot of happiness too—whether they are good or not," he reminded her. "This is a sad spot right here, but life isn't sad, you know, just because it is over—any more than music is. It takes a lot of happiness to make a life—anybody's life. Just imagine it—moonlight and wind and sleep, and the way things smell; and voices—and the way people feel about each other—" He looked at her standing there among the graves—*Nox est perpetua una dormienda.* "It takes a lot of happiness," he repeated, "for even a short life."

Anna was very quiet on the way home. She had hardly spoken since they left the graveyard—as they walked back to get on their horses and even after they had ridden out of the gate. "I hope those dogs will unearth something cheerful the next time," Hugh said. "Something like a moonshiner's hide-out."

"I wasn't thinking about that," she said. "I was remembering what you said about the things that make people happy—moonlight and things like that. I was wondering why everybody needs so much money all the time if they really only have to have what is free."

"Yes, but you see there is a catch in it," he said. "You have to be free yourself or you can't enjoy those things; lots of times you can't even have them; it's your own freedom that is expensive. Unless, of course, you just make up your mind to chuck everything and take to the woods—like Lo the poor Indian. It isn't as simple as it sounds—this question of money; it never has been simple. You have to strike a balance in there somewhere; neither too much nor too little; somewhere between Jay Gould and John Coujac, wouldn't you say? Or maybe somewhere around where you and Lawrence are going to be, say a year from now. He was talking about it too, the other day—about the best way for you all to spend your money. He seems to think if he just had a little more time than he has now, it would be about all he needs to make him happy." He turned to her, smiling. "You aren't short on time, are you? What do you need?"

"That's what I can't make out," she said.

"Doesn't that sound as if you must have just about everything already? That's bad, you know—to be happy and not know it. The best thing to do in a case like that is to begin imagining how you would feel if you had to do without things—what you might call counting your blessings by subtraction. I used to do that a lot. I can remember, when I was little, thinking how terrible it would be to have to give up—whatever it was, just to make myself enjoy having it that much more."

"What kind of things?—when you were little, I mean; before you began to notice about moonlight and voices and all those— wouldn't you call them spiritual things?"

"You mean more spiritual than a popgun or a jackknife? I'm not sure whether they can stand that comparison or not. I used to feel pretty spiritual about some of my possessions when I was little. I can't say I have ever stopped."

"I mean the opposite of material things," Anna explained. "I mean the things you enjoy with your mind."

"And not your body, which your dungeon is? Do you know that little poem?

> *My body, which my dungeon is,*
> *And yet my parks and palaces—*

It isn't a good idea to draw the line too close there, do you think so?"

"But I thought that was the thing that made the biggest difference in people—whether they liked spiritual things or material things the best."

"It does make a difference; what people like is about the best indication we have of what they are like themselves. I only mean you can't always be sure of what you ought to call it. It seems to me there are mighty few places a man ever wants to go where his body can't come along, and hardly be noticed most of the time. It's when he tries to make it go back that it begins to embarrass him—begins to howl like a puppy."

Anna did not smile. "I believe," he went on more seriously, "a good plan would be to work out—not a compromise exactly, but an understanding, that whenever we begin to notice the difference very much between what we call our physical side and what we think of as our spiritual side, it is a sign we have got on the wrong track. I don't believe we are meant to feel divided like that; certainly the more we seem to be all of a piece—all whole—the happier we are."

She did not say anything. He was not sure she was listening. "But you didn't want to hear all that," he said. "What was it you asked me?"

"It was about when you were little," she said; "but it doesn't matter. I was wondering what are some of the things that make you feel the way you said—that make you feel whole like that—besides religion, of course."

"Do they have to be 'besides'? Maybe religion is where they belong—what most of them are, in one way or another. Take beauty, for instance, and love—Wait a minute, I'll open it."

They went through the gate and he closed it behind them. They were at home now. "I believe we are going to have that rain," he said as they rode on to the house.

He had been thinking that the first rainy spell would be a good time for him to go over to New Orleans and look up some of the books he needed. Another thing his family did not understand about writing—at least about the kind of writing he was doing—was that most of it had been written already. They imagined him sitting over there on that porch like a bee among the blossoms—like a spider spinning in the blue air. They had not given a great deal of thought to those dry bones—

CHAPTER TEN

E HAD SAID he would not be gone more than a week. His mother may not have expected to see him back on the afternoon of the third day, but she did not seem surprised. They had all been so busy since the rain, she said.

"Anna has gone over to the Duncan place to take Uncle Mose the seed he has been waiting for," she told him. "This is the first afternoon she's been able to get out."

They both looked toward the gate.

"She ought to be back in a little while," Mrs. Martin said; "but you might ride on over if you feel like it."

She would be in the field, of course, he thought as he came in sight of the house. He would wait for her on the porch.

Then he saw her; she was sitting on the steps, as if she expected him to come; as if she might be waiting for him. He was almost frightened at the wave of happiness that swept over him.

"What made you think I was coming today?" he called to her, getting off of his horse and coming through the gate. "I didn't know it myself until just before I started. I meant to come tomorrow."

"How do you know I was not waiting for tomorrow?" she called back, laughing.

"It's been just dreadful without you, Hugh—the rain and everything. Do you know what I was thinking, sitting here?" she asked him.

He shook his head, standing before her at the foot of the steps.

"I was thinking about what you said the last time we rode home together—you remember—about how it made you appreciate things more to imagine having to give them up. I was imagining how I would feel if I knew you were not coming back—and then here you came! It works exactly like you said; I really am twice as glad to see you." She laughed again. It caught his breath to look at her.

"Are you ready to go? Have you finished?" he asked her. He was still standing; he must not sit down.

"Yes," she said; "but don't let's go quite yet. Sit down and let's admire our view, after all the rain. Do you realize this is our place, Hugh? It's the only thing we have ever done together in our lives."

He sat down a few steps below her and tried to look at the view—at anything. What had happened to him? Where had he been these three days, to have forgotten all that three years had taught him?

"And another thing I was doing," Anna said—"I was making myself miserable thinking you were going to find all sorts of things there in the library that would make you decide to go back to Richmond after you finish your book, instead of staying here. Lawrence said you wouldn't promise to do anything more than just think about it. How much longer do you have to think?"

Not any longer; he knew that now. A man did not have to think of the thing that was written in his forehead. It was there whether he thought of it or not. *Instead of staying here*—it came to him with a sudden clearness, a sudden steadiness, that there had never been anything instead of staying. They had talked as if he were free, and all the time they were binding him, putting garlands on him, leading him—to what green altar, O mysterious priest? He knew the altar; he had seen it lit by sun and moon and stars—all the tapers. He knew this god.

"Were you surprised to see me sitting here?" Anna asked him. "I suppose you can't imagine this porch without you on it, can you, Hugh? Isn't it always like that for the people who go away? They naturally don't think of themselves as gone, but just as being somewhere else—wherever it is they have gone to—don't they?"

"Who do you mean by people?" Hugh asked her. "If you mean me—if it is my mind you are reading—you are doing a very poor job; worse than your gypsy. I always leave so much of myself behind me when I go away that I hardly have enough left to do anything with in the place I have gone to. I wonder you all don't see me around sometimes, acting as if I were still here."

"I did once—don't you remember?" Anna said. "You said it was a—something in German—bad luck, you said."

"That's a fact; you did—my *Doppelgänger*. Well, that ought to prove something, don't you think so?"

"Maybe it only proves it about me," she said. "But anyhow I don't believe you are going."

He stood up. "Just now we both are," he said, "so come on."

He could not understand it—the feeling of triumph that suddenly possessed him now that he had given up the struggle. He was all at once completely happy, completely sure. Riding home with Anna through the sunset, though he was conscious every moment of an altered relation between them, not once did it present itself as being due to any failure on his part; there was no sense of wrong in any direction, no sense of loss. Surely he could not be so lost himself that he would welcome anything, even his own weakness, rather than fight any longer against the odds that had become too strong for him? He could not be deceived like that; he might be reconciled to defeat, but he could not mistake it for victory. It seemed to him that he stood on the brink of some ineffable initiation—some conversion of the spirit by which all that was weakest in him and all that was strongest would be shown to be the same.

The days that followed, and especially the nights, were filled with such premonitions. The thing required of him was submission—the quiet acceptance of the laws of his own soul. What right did he have to suppose he could set them aside as he had tried to do, and then expect to be at peace? A man was a fool to put his own will between himself and what had been ordained for him. The end of a thing was its nature; he did not need Aristotle to teach him that. And what hope could there be of attaining the unity he had always set above everything—that he had held as the very foundation of happiness—if he could not be at one with his own destiny? If he could not learn to conform his changes to its changelessness—to love it as himself?

> *They reason ill who leave me out;*
> *When me they fly, I am the wings—*

No wonder he had lost his way—groping in ignorance as he had done. He began to feel a sort of sorrow for himself—his blindness, his vanity—all the waste of effort they had caused him. No injunction had been laid upon him to renounce the passion of his youth; he saw that now; the denial of love was not exacted from any living thing—how could it be? He would be judged only by the manner of his acceptance—no longer in the blindness of youth nor with youth's fantastic claims, but with a man's understanding—as the meaning of life itself; as the thing most beautiful and strongest against death. He was enraptured by this new sense of the forces within him. Dying might turn out to be like this, he thought—to wake up and find you had everything again and knew the way to keep it.

He found himself wondering, as the days passed, whether Anna noticed the difference in him; whether she saw how much happier he was, how much more free. He could say things to her now that he would not have said even a few days ago. There was no fear in the love he had for her now; how could there be, when there was no longer any hope? Everywhere he looked he saw only certainty—the certainty of himself.

Whether Anna noticed a difference in him or not, she made no effort to conceal the fact that there was one in her; it grew plainer every day. She wanted to be with him more than she had ever done before; to listen to him, and even to talk to him, especially about the past—that past when she had hardly talked at all.

"I remember you as such a quiet little girl," he said to her one day. "Were you—or have I just forgotten? It seems to me Lawrence and I used to do all the talking. Certainly we made all the noise; I can't remember anything we said."

"I remember some of it," Anna said. "I remember I used always to be on Lawrence's side. You seemed to be so much older; it is only lately that I have begun to catch up with you. Lawrence stopped being afraid of you long before I did."

"When did you stop?" he asked her, smiling. "This is all something I didn't know about; I'm interested."

She thought a little. "I'm just stopping now. I used to take spells of being less afraid of you, but I always went back. Now you seem more—" She hesitated; not because she was afraid of him, though; he felt sure of that.

"So if I can just stay as I am," he said after waiting awhile for her to continue, "you think you won't go back and be afraid of me again? You can't imagine how funny that seems to me—the idea of you, or Lawrence either, standing in awe of me."

She did not answer. They were sitting on the steps again, ready to go but not going; talking about their past.

"Do you remember, Hugh," she asked him after a while, "what that gypsy said about you having a dark face?—a dark face and many thoughts, was what she said; and I have been wondering whether you look that way even when your thoughts are pleasant—look dark, I mean."

At the moment he was looking puzzled; then he said : "Oh, I see—you don't think she was referring to my complexion; you are determined to get a meaning into it somehow, aren't you?"

"But I have always noticed it, Hugh," she said earnestly. "That is one of the reasons I used to be afraid of you—the way your face changes so; and the way I could never tell which it was going to be."

"Which is it now?" he asked, turning it to her.

This time she smiled. "I am not going to tell you!" she said. "All I mean is I have learned now that lots of times when you look like that, it is over something maybe a thousand miles away, that doesn't have anything to do with anybody."

He shook his head. "Not that far away, I'm afraid. The most fantastic things we can imagine have to be made out of the things we know already. That is why they hardly ever turn out to be so different from reality; they are just a little more permanent, maybe, but otherwise pretty much what we are used to."

She thought this over, looking at him all the time, as if that made his meaning clearer.

"Isn't that funny!" she said. "I never thought of it before—the way people talk as if imaginary things were so perishable, and the others were the ones they could keep; and it is really just the other way, isn't it? Maybe your dreams don't have to go through that hourglass—you remember you told me—the way your real life has to do."

"That's it exactly," he said. "We are *not* the stuff that dreams are made on—Shakespeare said we were, you know, but he was mistaken—and so we have to dream."

Anna did not say anything. She was thinking of something else. "Do you know, Hugh," she said after a while, "I used to wonder sometimes—" She stopped; she was looking at him, but not, he thought, as he was now; she was seeing him somewhere in the past again.

"Go on," he said encouragingly; he did not want to stay in the past. "What did you use to wonder? Was it some more about me—whether I was really as bad as I looked?"

She shook her head; she would not go on; not even back into those long-ago days when everything had been so safe for them; when they had even been safe from one another.

As for that later time when they had not been safe—the paths that might have led them there had been so long disused as to be wellnigh obliterated. They never spoke of that abolished kingdom; its laws, its language, were alike forgotten. If they talked of love now, it was not that love.

"Do you remember, Hugh," she asked him, "when we were riding home that day—it was the day we found the graveyard—and you said it always made you happier if you could feel as if you were the same all through, instead of being part good and part bad?"

"I remember," he said.

"And you said love was one of the things that made people feel that way."

"I remember," he said again.

"Yes, but did you mean that was because to love somebody very much made you stop thinking about yourself any more?" Anna asked him. "Or would it be because if somebody loved you the way you wanted her to, then that would keep you from wanting anything else? It could work either of those ways, couldn't it?"

"It could," he said—"or both of them. Both at the same time would be the ideal arrangement, wouldn't it? It's an old question—does love want to give everything, or take everything? Is love a prince or a beggar? Arguments like that never are settled because as a rule nobody is talking about the same thing."

"But which did you mean?" she asked him.

"I meant—" he paused a moment. "I hope I meant something like a confession of faith; like believing the spring would come, or the resurrection. Love can be like that, you know—for this body of our death—when we believe it."

She did not say anything; she sat very still, her eyes on his face, like some one lost in listening, until presently—"We must go," she said, getting up, and they went down the steps together.

"Did you ever think, Hugh," Anna asked him on another afternoon, "how everything bad that has ever happened to us—to you or to me either—has always been when we were in town and never in the country? There was that Christmas—it was the first Christmas after you went to New Orleans—and you wouldn't come home because that man at Garibaldi's had the smallpox and you were afraid you might give it to us; and then of course that time in Richmond—"

"And you—" he prompted, to help her out of Richmond— "what ever happened to you in town that wasn't nice? I can't seem to remember anything."

"Don't you remember about my arm—that summer when I came back from Mobile with it in a sling because the doctor thought it was broken?"

"That's a fact, you did. And it turned out to be a mistake, didn't it? Or maybe the country cured it right away. I know you didn't wear the sling very long or I would have remembered it." Hugh was smiling at her, but she didn't seem to notice it.

"What I mean is that the disagreeable things always seem to happen away from home," Anna said. "Of course," she added reflectively, "there was Mr. Leeroy; that was about as disagreeable as anything could be, just as an experience, and yet even that turned out to be so different; it is almost as if he had actually done me a favor by behaving the way he did—so really ruffianly; because if you all hadn't been afraid for me to come over here by myself, all this—" she looked about her; at the porch where they were sitting, at the horses waiting for them by the gate, at Hugh's writing table, and at Hugh—"not any of it, really," she said, "would ever have happened. You would be back in Richmond writing on your book, and I would still be coming over here by myself the way I started out to do. So, as far as I'm concerned, Mr. Leeroy has turned out to be a blessing in disguise."

They both laughed at this; then Anna went on, seriously: "How much more have you got to write, Hugh? I mean *about* how much? Lawrence says I mustn't try to pin you down—about your book, or about staying here, or anything; Lawrence isn't as sure as I am that you are going to stay." She searched his face with her beautiful eyes; she did not look sure. "And of course I know why," she said. "It's because he is so unselfish; he doesn't think about having his own way all the time. Lawrence has always been unselfish."

"And Anna hasn't? I remember her as a very unselfish little girl."

"Maybe once," she said. "But now I can't even imagine giving up anything I want as bad as this; though of course I want you to want it too. If I could even be sure of that—"

"But how can you not be sure?" he said. "How can you think I—" He stopped.

"Then you will?" she cried, springing to her feet. "And we can tell the others you have really decided? Oh, Hugh, it is going to be so wonderful! Like having the past come back." Her face was radiant. Before he could gather up his books or his briefcase, she was on her way to the gate.

The weather had been very warm. Not the kind of heat that induces resignation; it was too early in the year for that; but the kind that promises a change. Every afternoon the clouds would gather over Anna's fields and Uncle Mose would tell the boys to "hurry up now befo' it starts rainin' "; and Hugh, viewing the same phenomena from his porch, would begin to hurry too, putting things together, getting ready to start the moment he saw Anna coming. Then every afternoon nothing would happen; the clouds would only move to other fields and he and Anna would ride home as usual through the long shadows under a clear sky.

He had been back from New Orleans about a week and they had reached what was admittedly their hottest day when one afternoon, with surprising suddenness, things took a different turn. Before he had even begun to collect his papers they were already blowing along the porch; before he had time to look for Anna he saw her rounding the thicket at a gallop, her hat flying back from her shoulders, her skirt gone wild with the wind.

She was at the gate before he reached it. "I'll put them in the stable," he called to her as she slid down from the saddle. "Run for it!"

The rain had begun by the time he got back to the porch. They could not sit on the steps; they pushed the table back against the wall and sat on that.

"Did you ever see anything so sudden!" Anna said. "We were just finishing when that black cloud came up, exactly as if we had ordered it for the potato slips. Do you reckon Uncle Mose and the boys made it to the shed?"

"What do we do if they didn't?" he asked her. "You might have allowed them a little more time, though."

"Well, anyhow, let's enjoy it," Anna said. "When you talk about the lovely things people have in their lives, it seems to me you leave out the loveliest one of all if you don't mention rain— when you need it, of course. It is not only the way it sounds but the way it smells—" she inhaled luxuriously.

"How about the way it feels?" he said, getting off of the table and picking up his briefcase. "Come on, we'll have to go in."

The wind had begun whipping the rain in on them, and Anna's protest, coinciding as it did with a roll of thunder, was inaudible even to her.

It was the first time she had been inside the house since the spring began; the box she had sat on to warm her feet was still there at the corner of the hearth. She did not sit on it now; she went over and stood by the window where she could watch the storm.

Hugh went over and stood by it too, where he could watch her. Anna's behavior in a storm had always been memorable; she was one of those who looked on tempests and was never shaken.

It was not late; it would be another hour before sunset; but except for the blinding flashes of lightning it had grown almost dark. If they were at home somebody would be sure to light a lamp to do something by. They did not have one here and would not have lighted it if they had; there was not anything to do. They had even stopped talking on account of the thunder. Anna's face against the glass of the window, alternately dark and pale with the play of the sky outside, was more like the moon than ever.

"Goodness! I think that got one of the trees, Hugh," she exclaimed after the worst bolt yet had fallen. She was trying to see out, pressing her forehead against the pane.

"Come back from the window!" He put out his arm to draw her back, and drew her to his breast.

She held her white face up to meet his face, and they stood there together with the lightning round them, in an empty house, an empty world.

Silence returned and found them there, as still as if they never meant to move again. Time too returned, and thought— and destiny, which he had trusted and which had betrayed him. He raised his face to the window; his arms fell at his sides.

"I have no way to keep from loving you, Anna. I will have to go," he said.

"But not without me, Hugh—you don't mean that?" Anna's voice trembled a little. "Aren't we both going as soon as it stops raining enough?"

"I don't mean home," he said. "I mean away—somewhere where I can't see you. I thought I was stronger than I am—I thought it was only for myself—"

"But it will never be like this again, Hugh—it never was before. You know we could go on forever with nothing like this again—"

He looked at her in silence by the returning light. Outside the clouds were breaking on a rain-washed sky.

"It must have been the lightning," she went on earnestly. "It seemed for those few minutes—those few seconds—as if we were the only people in the world. But surely you don't think you have to go away on account of that! I can promise you—I can promise everybody—never to feel like that again—not if you stay and help me, Hugh."

"But I can't help you, Anna; you see that. I can't even help myself. We can go now; the rain has almost stopped."

"But promise me, Hugh—promise me now before we start—that you are not going away just because we love each other! Maybe we have been doing it all the time without knowing it—without me knowing it. Nobody ever told me it could be like this. I thought love was supposed to make you happy; I didn't know that anybody ever felt this way—"

"Come, Anna," he said, "come out on the porch. I will get the horses. We can talk about it after you have had more time to think."

"But I can't unless you promise," she said. "I can't think about anything except not wanting you to go away!"

"You can think about Lawrence," he said. "We can both do that."

Mrs. Middleton refused to take anything but a cheerful view of Hugh's decision to go back to Richmond. It had a bright side, she told his mother, and even if it hadn't, Hugh was old enough to know what he ought to do about his own business. Richmond was not as far away as a lot of other places, and a young man, in her opinion, was better off away from home until he had a home of his own. The bachelor son—the bachelor brother—practically every family in the South had one of them around, and for her part she had always felt sorry for him. Naturally he was better fed at home, and had his socks all darned and his buttons sewed on, but Hugh could still come back often enough for her to patch him up and see that he did not lose too much weight. Mrs. Spottswood probably had a new cook by this time anyhow.

So much for the side she turned persistently toward Louisa; if she did not mention some other aspects of the matter, it was not because she viewed them with less approval, but because no one had mentioned them to her. She had been left to find her way as best she could through a good deal of ambiguity with regard to what had been going on of late both at Nutwood and at the Duncan place.

Whatever it was, she would be glad when Hugh was out of it. That idea of his staying had seemed to her preposterous from the first; it fairly reeked with catastrophe.—Sensible people too; practical. There were a lot of practical perils lying around for people who didn't do any dreaming. That family would have gone on the rocks before this if they hadn't had something like Hugh in their midst. It really takes a poet to stand up to life on anything like equal terms, when you come right down to it; it is probably always disastrous not to be a poet. Take poor little Anna, for instance. A lot of things must have been left out of Anna to start with—to make room for her looks. There was something primordial about her; she didn't seem to have inherited anything from her maternal ancestors. It was almost, Mrs. Middleton thought, as if Anna had to work out the business of being a woman for herself; the first one ever made; poor motherless Eve. She had not been feeling the same about Anna since the day of their last interview—the day of the blush. She realized that instead of blaming her she ought really to be saying some kind of prayer for her; only she didn't know exactly how to word it. She had been watching Anna for so long, bringing this thing on herself; it seemed unreasonable to turn around and ask for it not to happen. Mrs. Middleton was surprised to find herself feeling so much like God. Only He probably didn't expect prayers to be reasonable; He was too used to the other kind. O Lord, avert the course of justice! Call off the Eumenides! And poor little Anna, with no more imagination than a rabbit—

As far as she herself was concerned, Mrs. Middleton was well aware that whatever form her sympathy or her prayers should take, there was no use in expecting anything much in the way of confidence to be reposed in her from this time on. She would probably never be told anything more than she knew at present about what had actually happened to influence Hugh's decision. It was of course possible that he had never as seriously considered staying as the others had considered it for him; and certainly it was more than possible—it was true—that he needed, as Louisa said, a more "literary atmosphere"; these assumptions were there for everybody to use; they were already wearing thin in places; thin enough to see through. For something *had* happened, and in spite of the fact that Hugh was not leaving suddenly, Mrs. Middleton was convinced that the decision had been sudden— and that it had been Anna.

He was not leaving suddenly. Decently and in order; there was no danger of everything not being kept in its place, as usual. And no matter how many times she might see Hugh before he left, the little he would tell her would not give her much more to go on than she had now. Ask me no questions and I'll tell you no lies.

Hugh might indeed have been more than ever disposed to endorse this local aphorism—feeling as he did that too many of the questions he had asked himself of late should have had other answers given them. He wondered a good deal during these last days, both at what he had promised and at what he had believed—this show of faith that could so plausibly move moun- tains. The light had changed now; the play was over; the music and belief had died. All that was left now was for the fallen hero to pick himself up and come before the curtain to explain the piece. It was like this, he would say. The epilogue; unreasonable as it might seem to make up words about what you had seen with your eyes, had looked upon and your hands had handled—still, you always did.

He kept going back to the beginning—even farther back than that. What lay behind it all? How much of what a man did depended on himself and not on what others had done for him— long ago perhaps; over and over, until it had got into his blood, into his senses—like the horn of Roland—so that he obeyed before he thought—before he could even hear? He had not had time for thinking—standing there in the midst of the lightning, holding the world in his arms, the sea cupped in his hands. Something had to be there already. To have come up against himself as he had done and been convinced of his own powerlessness was an experience he could not afford to forget. He wanted to keep hold of that other resource that had been revealed to him—to get it somehow into the continuity of his life.

"Sometimes it seems to me," he said to Anna on one of those last days, "that the past is more binding on us than anything. There is no telling what we would do with the present, or the future, if we could forget what they have cost already—what other people have had to pay, I mean, and the sacrifices they have had to make to leave things even as nice as they are. Don't you remember what you said, that time when we were over there in the graveyard, about how hard it must be for people to go on being good when they are unhappy?"

"But I do want to be good, Hugh; you know I do! I just can't see anything wrong in your staying here where we can see each other, the way we have done all our lives. I can't see how that can possibly hurt Lawrence or anybody. You say we have to think about him, and I do; but I never did think about Lawrence all the time."

The epilogue was always an old story, because the play itself was old. It had to have a pattern or it couldn't be a play. The place, for instance—no matter how far away they put it, it would be a place you knew, that you could describe, as Anna's gypsy had described Nutwood; you would always see the familiar windows, and the roof, and the make-believe towers—the things you had always seen.

Nutwood was supposed to have been built away from everything—even the little world his father and mother had lived in; they wanted it to be different; they had drowned it in the woods—lost Lyoness—yet there it was—a house, ugly and comfortable, full of leafy sunlight and silence and the sounds that all meant something—that you listened for. Jug and bed and candle; peace and peril—Agamemnon's house had those things, and Iseult's. People lived there; it was home. They worked there; making, doing, from morning until night; always striving for something—for more of what they had already; there was no something-else. Not to work for; the other things were free—beauty and love and sorrow—the dangerous things. They were the action, they were the play. They were what the living died for, and why the dead returned.

In which case, crossing the Styx would be no better for him than going to Richmond. Wherever he went he would always come back. The question now was what he would bring with him—or take away.

"But how can it be taking anything away from Lawrence?" Anna said. "I never felt like this before about anybody. It happened before I knew it—"

"Maybe it will go before you know it, too," he said.

She shook her head. "It can't; it is like learning something that you never knew; there isn't any way not to know it after that." Anna's eyes with her new knowledge in them made the last days hard.

"Lawrence doesn't see any difference—he doesn't know that anything has happened—that I have changed at all," she said.

"But he will know. Lawrence likes whole things too. Certainly he wants you whole—not cut up into little stars, like Romeo. You haven't had time to think about it yet," Hugh told her.

"Have you been thinking very long?" she asked.

"Ever since I can remember," he said, "so, you see, I ought to know."

He was smiling, but Anna did not even try to smile. "I just can't bear it; that is all," she said in a low voice.

He waited before he spoke again—waited until she took her eyes away; there was something he had to tell her—something he knew she had not thought of and might not be willing to consider now; but he must try.

"Do you know what we mean by that—when we say we can't bear something?" he asked her.

She shook her head, but not, he thought, entirely in despair, so he went on.

"In almost every case it means we have found out we are paying too much for it—that in one way or another—pain, sacrifice—it is costing us more than we can afford. Some things are like that, you know; we go on paying for them and yet they can never belong to us. I don't want you to pay too much for this—for feeling this way about me. The time might come when you would rather I would stay away. No—don't—I will never do it unless you want me to—look at the way I have kept on coming all these years!"

He made her look at it—at the past, which seemed so long to both of them, and at the future, which seemed still so free. "Don't you remember what you said?" he asked her—"that there are always so many things that can happen in the future? Think about some of them now."

Anna listened. She had dried her tears; she was thinking of something in the future that she was sure he had forgotten—

"It was what the gypsy said," she reminded him—"about how you were going to live at Nutwood *toujours*—and about the little boy who would look just like you. Had you forgotten that?"

"No," he said, "not even that. Not anything."